*The*
## PETTICOAT PARTY

# Gold-Rush Phoebe

*The*
# PETTICOAT PARTY
*Series*:

Book 1: GO WEST, YOUNG WOMEN!
Book 2: PHOEBE'S FOLLY
Book 3: OREGON, SWEET OREGON
Book 4: GOLD-RUSH PHOEBE

*The*
# PETTICOAT PARTY
*Book 4*

# Gold-Rush
# Phoebe

# KATHLEEN KARR

J
Karr

**HarperTrophy®**
*A Division of HarperCollinsPublishers*

Gold-Rush Phoebe

Library of Congress Cataloging-in-Publication Data
Karr, Kathleen.
    Gold-rush Phoebe / Kathleen Karr.
    p.        cm. — (The Petticoat Party ; bk. 4)
    Summary: In 1848, fifteen-year-old Phoebe Brown disguises herself as a
boy and runs away with her friend Robbie Robson to join in the California
gold rush and, after many adventures, they eventually find themselves
running a restaurant in San Francisco.
    ISBN 0-06-440498-6 (pbk.)
    [1. Runaways—Fiction.    2. Gold mines and mining—Fiction.
3. Sex role—Fiction.    4. Business enterprises—Fiction.    5. San Francisco
(Calif.)—Fiction.    6. California—History—1846–1850—Fiction.]
I. Title.    II. Series: Karr, Kathleen. Petticoat Party ; bk. 4.
PZ7.K149Gp    1998                                                97-39279
[Fic]—dc21                                                            CIP
                                                                          AC

1  2  3  4  5  6  7  8  9  10
❖
First Edition

For Larry, Suzanne, and Daniel—
thank you for the trips, and the memories!

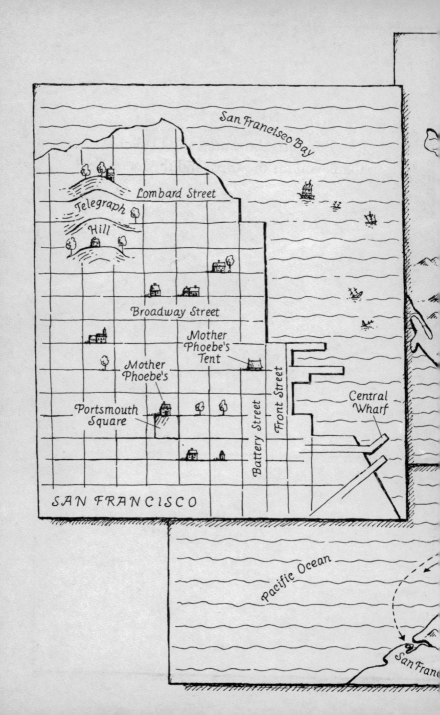

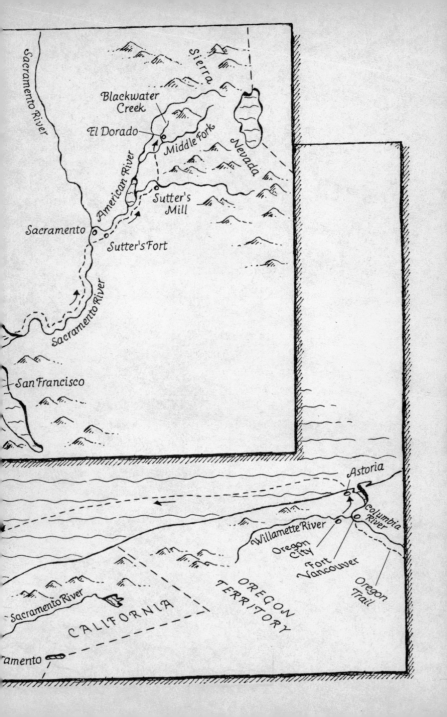

*The*

# PETTICOAT PARTY

# Gold-Rush Phoebe

# ONE

*J*ust before boarding the boat I was shorn. It made me feel like some kind of sacrificial lamb.

"You planning on offering me up on an altar next, Robbie? The same as Abraham and Isaac?"

"You're already way too tough for that, Phoebe." Robbie kept hacking away with his knife, seeming to take a grim satisfaction in the operation. "Anyhow, we talked it out, remember? There's no way you can keep all this hair tucked up under your pa's old slouch hat. You want to run away after gold, you've got to act like a boy. You want to be taken for a boy, you've got to look like one. You've got to give up something." He whacked off one more luxurious handful and sank back next to our small campfire, studying the hank in his grasp. "I sort of like this reddish-brown color."

"Auburn, Robbie. It's called auburn."

"Closer to a bay, I'd say."

I groaned. "You sound just like Mr. Harley back

at Fort Laramie. Next thing, you'll be comparing me to your favorite horse."

Robbie grinned. "Can't say I ever had that kind of attachment to a horse, Phoebe." He slowly tied the hank into a knot with his big hands, then shoved it into his pack.

"Hey! What are you doing with my hair?"

"Only a keepsake, Phoebe. To remember these times by."

"It's gold you should be thinking to fill that pack with, Robbie Robson, not keepsakes."

"Gold isn't all that glitters," he murmured.

I let the comment pass to feel for what was left of my precious hair. Fifteen years—my entire life—it had been growing. Now it was mostly gone. How could a boy begin to understand how that felt? Even an eighteen-year-old young man like Robbie? Well, maybe his keeping that hank said something for him—one of those somethings being that he secretly harbored other ideas about the two of us than just a straight-out gold-seeking partnership. For such a big, hefty farm boy, Robbie had surprised me with a whole bunch of things already on this trip. If it made him happy to squirrel away a bit of my lost hair, that was all right with me. My disguise and Robbie's shyness would be protection enough against any other ideas. *Adventure* was our true mission.

At the time of my shearing we'd been on the road for California and the gold rush for five days. But the road wasn't much in these parts. Mostly, it wasn't even a trail. We'd just kept pushing our way north from Oregon City, following the Willamette River till it emptied into the broad Columbia, stopping only long enough to hunt a rabbit or two for the supper fire. We bypassed Fort Vancouver, just in case word had gotten out about my escape.

Mama knew I'd taken off from the homestead, of course, even knew where Robbie and I were bound. She probably figured that my practice in survival on the Oregon Trail with the Petticoat Party would stand me in good stead. But Papa was another matter entirely. Especially with me leaving him shorthanded on the farm. Once Mama revealed my plans to him—as she was bound to— Papa was capable of dropping everything to track me down and haul me home again. So it was not in my best interest to bump into my big sister Amelia's former beau at Fort Vancouver. Mr. Hugh Montague Montmorency Croft struck me as a telltale sort of person.

Once on the Columbia, Robbie and I had proceeded west along its banks, making for Astoria and the ships we hoped to meet there heading for California and the gold fields.

Gold. You could get rich if you found it, but you couldn't find it without some kind of a money stake to get you to California in the first place. It was an interesting dilemma, like an old mutt chasing after its tail. I suppose I was feeling a trifle insecure without even a penny to my name, so Robbie and I had discussed money right from the start.

"How're we going to book passage on a ship without money, Robbie?" I asked that the very first morning of the trip, not three miles north of home. We'd taken a break to rest by the edge of the river, our backs hemmed in by the great forests trying on their autumn colors.

"Not to worry." Sprawled out against his pack, he patted his stomach, right over a small lump under his shirt. "I've still got my enlistment money from the Cayuse Wars. My ma sewed it into a little belt for me, for safekeeping."

"That's fine for you, but I served my enlistment on my papa's homestead. And Papa never did pay out a wage to family members."

"Don't fuss, Phoebe. We're partners, ain't we? We'll share."

"You'd do that?"

"I took you on as a partner. What's mine is yours now. Share and share alike."

I considered Robbie's generosity as we eased up from our rest and trekked another half mile along the river. "There might not be enough for passage for both of us. And then there'll be equipment to buy once we get to California—"

"Exactly. So I figure what we have to do is work out our passage."

"As sailors? I've never even been on a boat, Robbie—aside from the Linn City ferry and another few coming west from Massachusetts."

"It won't matter if we're willing. And I'm willing."

I lapsed into silence, just concentrating on getting the hang of Papa's trousers. They sure did feel strange rubbing against my legs the way they did. His old blue woolen shirt was kind of scratchy against my skin, too. But at least it was baggy enough to hide my other female attributes. That and his mangiest old vest hid a lot of sins. A final thought occurred to me.

"What if they don't need any help aboard ship, Robbie?"

I turned to see his reaction. It was a wide grin.

"Why, then, we'll just smuggle ourselves aboard, Phoebe."

"You mean like stowaways?"

"Exactly."

So here we were at the village of Astoria, where the Columbia burst out into the Pacific Ocean. It was deep night and dark. Good for our plans, but not necessarily for a modish haircut. Robbie took one more swipe at my hair and gave up.

"It'll do, I reckon." He tucked his knife into the sheath hanging from his leather belt. "It's surely pitiful enough for someone to take mercy on you if we're discovered."

"Too bad the ship didn't need any help."

We'd tried, fair and square, earlier in the afternoon. The captain of the sole vessel in port had only laughed. "With everybody and his brother wanting to ship for California? Show me your gold, boys, and ye can ride my fine brigantine like the others," he'd said.

Now the deck of the brig was littered with sleeping bodies, paying passengers all. It would sail with the tide. I felt once more where my hair should've been and shrugged. "Tide's coming in, Robbie. We'd best do the deed."

We snuffed out the fire, shouldered our packs, and scurried like rats toward the darkest side of the brig. The gangplank had already been pulled up, probably to discourage others like us. We'd seen them around the small port that afternoon. Full-grown men seemingly poorer than us, hungrily eyeing the *Oriental*. But Robbie and I, we were determined as well as hungry for California. We were younger and more reckless, too. Neither the lack of passage money nor lack of a welcoming gangplank would keep us from that ship.

The hull of the *Oriental* was grinding against the timbers of the wharf. I halted to stare up its steep sides. There wasn't anything for a hand or toe to grasp. Nothing except a few heavy ropes falling from the deck above.

"Catch onto one of those ropes and start hoisting yourself up, Phoebe!" Robbie's whisper came urgently to my ears. "And when you get over the top, tuck under some of those piled-up sails!"

I gave the ropes another assessment. I had brought this upon myself, after all. I'd been so all-fired anxious for a little freedom and liberty from the farm, for a little adventure. Scaling hulls, apparently, came under the heading of adventure. And if I didn't act soon and fast, I'd have Robbie and me both caught. I grabbed at the rough hemp with all my might. Robbie gave me an unexpected boost with strong hands firmly planted on my rear quarters. Boots toeing the hull, I climbed, hand over hand. I fell over the top with a gasp. I'd landed directly on some paying passenger's legs!

"Watch yer boots!" he growled, before turning over in his bedroll.

Heart thumping, I directed my feet around other bodies as quietly as possible, making for a vast pile of sails near the smaller mast. In a moment I was burrowing beneath its safety. I heard another, louder growl. Robbie must've landed on the same poor soul. Then he was burrowing next to me.

"You made it!"

"Hush," he murmured. "I just missed the captain himself coming on deck."

We lay shrouded in the heavy cloth, catching our breaths, praying our ploy might work. Gradually sounds of the awakening ship filtered through. Clanking boots, ropes being cast off, sails being raised. My heart stopped again. What if there was a need for these very sails now sheltering us? What if . . . but the ship had begun a heavier rocking. Creaking oars signified it was being towed away from the wharf. There were indistinguishable orders barked out and obeyed, then a different motion overtook the ship as wind caught the sails. We were under way. We were actually under way!

*Thank you, Lord.* Next stop, California! The gentle motion slowly overtook my exhausted body. I drifted off to sleep.

Fresh air, sea spray, and blinding sunlight hit me all at once. I opened my eyes.

"Bloody barnacles! A land rat! Two of them!"

I froze in terror as the swarthy face of a sailor met my gaze.

"Captain! Captain Fallows! Stowaways!"

"What? What's going on?" Robbie rubbed his eyes beside me and shifted upright on his elbows. "What happened to the sails?"

"Gone, Robbie. We've been discovered." Now that my eyes were fully open, however, my fright disappeared. Any fool could see we were clear out in the middle of the Pacific Ocean. What could the captain do to us, after all? He wasn't likely to turn back to restore us to the land, and he couldn't very well toss us overboard, either. I grinned. "It's the ocean at last, Robbie! And it's as grand as we thought!"

Robbie wasn't enjoying the sight precisely as I was. That sailor had caught him by the scruff of his neck and was currently hauling him to his feet. In another moment, a second sailor had my own neck in a viselike grip, raising my entire body above the deck, shaking me as he would a true rat.

"Hang on, Phoe—Feeb—" Robbie managed to croak out. "Just hang on."

Wasn't much else I could do. I hung, suspended, as the ship lurched with the wind, tacking through an impressive wave, its square-rigged sails billowing. I finally swayed sideways in my captor's grasp. My boots touched the deck again as I caught sight of the captain heading our way. He arrived sooner than I'd have liked, an alarming figure, indeed. Captain Fallows was squat and solid on his feet, with a leer on his thick lips that I hadn't noticed the afternoon before.

"What have we here? By my troth, the two young men with a taste for gold but no passage money!" He rubbed at his graying side-whiskers, and his bushy gray eyebrows rose frighteningly beneath the visor of his cap as he bared his teeth at us.

My throat was a mite constricted at the moment, as it was still being clenched in a fairly tight grip, but I managed to spit out something anyhow. "We'll work! . . . We've always been willing to work!"

The captain nodded sharply to my tormentor, and I was loosed. "Ye, with the soft face. Ye own a name?"

"Phoeb—, uh, Feeb Brown," I gasped, reaching for my sorely tried neck muscles. "The Feeb stands for F. B. . . . Francis Benedict," I embroidered.

Robbie struggled within his own captor's hold to straighten his impressive length. "I am Robert Sturdevant Robson."

Sturdevant? Where'd that come from? Maybe Robbie was just trying to match me. If I'd known he was going to outdo me, though, I could've come up with a much more impressive handle. The thought fled as my neck was caught again. Captain Fallows's smile had turned even more sinister.

"Ye both have freely chosen to put yourself under my command, and that of the Law of the Sea." He nodded at our captors. "We needed some entertainment anyway. The seas are too calm."

The ship lurched through another colossal wave and I reeled with it, feeling suddenly grateful for my empty stomach. This was calm?

"The mast and the cat-o'-nine-tails," the captain barked. "Strip 'em to their breeches and give 'em five lashes each. Then down to the hold for both of them. Bread and water only till California."

I gulped. It wasn't even the lashes part. I figured I could stand up to that almost as well as any young man. It was the stripping part beforehand that had me worried.

"Sir!" Robbie was suddenly ramrod stiff, and I could see the soldier part of him for the first time. "Sir! Stowing away was my idea, not my cousin's. He is frail. Allow me to take his punishment for him."

"Ten lashes?" The captain's eyebrows rose further. "The best of men cannot take ten lashes."

"Sir! I beg you favor me with this boon."

The captain spat—just to the left of Robbie's boots—then grinned. "Very well. It might be interesting."

It was hard watching Robbie take that punishment for me. It was scary, too. I'd truly had no idea of what was involved. It was worse than the buffalo massacre two and a half years back on the Oregon Trail. I'd only seen the aftereffects of that catastrophe. This one I had to attend. But Robbie was true-blue and foursquare.

The hardest moment was just before the punishment began, after all the paying passengers had gathered in a silent circle around the mainmast to oversee Captain Fallows's entertainment. Robbie's shirt was roughly torn from his shoulders to hang loose just above his waist, just above his money belt. Would the belt be discovered? And why hadn't Robbie offered its contents in payment when we were caught? I was beginning to learn he had a hidden stubborn streak. That money had been earmarked for mining supplies, and he'd not relinquish it for anything else, even to escape a flogging.

I closed my eyes as the iron-tipped claws of the whip lashed out against his bare back the first time. Then I forced them open. If Robbie could bear his and my punishment both, then I could at least be strong enough to watch it. Anything else would be sheer cowardice.

*Help him, Lord,* I prayed. *Give him strength. Give me strength, too.*

The whip struck again and again, each stroke timed agonizingly for shifts of the ship between waves. Robbie clung to the mainmast till his sun-browned fingers turned white, but he uttered not a sound. Suddenly I knew that our fine adventure was not going to be as easy as anticipated.

Robbie and I never got to see any gamboling otters or whales like we'd talked about way back in Oregon City. We never got more than that one morning's glimpse of the Pacific Ocean. The next five days were spent in a boxed-off section of the hold, atop stacks of lumber and barrels of newly harvested Oregon Territory grain being shipped south.

"Wouldn't it be funny if we were sitting on some of my papa's precious wheat, Robbie?"

Robbie moaned. I was the one sitting. He was still stretched out flat on his stomach atop his bedroll. At least the captain had had the courtesy to toss our packs down the hole after us when we'd been incarcerated. Our packs and a whale-oil lantern, but not my rifle. Papa's rifle, truly. Papa would not be pleased by this turn of events.

Since then we'd seen nothing but hardtack and stagnant water, twice a day. The sailor doing the provisioning had had mercy on Robbie, though. With the first evening's allotment he'd handed me a jar of thick, black, greasy stuff.

"For your friend's back," he whispered. "Don't let on, or I'll be for the cat, too. But that old devil Fallows won't have me for long. Not after we dock in San Francisco. Not with the gold fields calling. He'll be sailing thereafter with only his Law of the Sea for hands, I'll voucher."

"Thank you, and God bless you!" I meant it, too. The sailor disappeared and I began tending to Robbie.

It was an educational experience nursing Robbie's wounds. For the first time I began to understand my big sister Amelia's attentions to her printer Wade Jennings when he'd been so sick last

Christmas, before he'd finally proposed marriage. I'd never taken myself for any kind of ministering angel, but Robbie surely needed help, and it was warm and comforting giving it to him. Amazing how he'd stood up for me like that. Now it was my turn to stand up for him. We were partners, after all.

It wasn't till the second day in the hold that he started talking again.

"Lord, Phoebe, but your fingers are cool on my burning skin. Please don't stop. . . . But how can you stand it? It must look as bad as it feels."

"Don't fret, Robbie. Couldn't any of you look bad to me after what you did. Just concentrate on getting better. You'll need to be healthy when we arrive."

He groaned and twisted under my touch. "I guess I had it coming, anyhow. There ain't nothing free in life, no matter how you look at it, Phoebe."

"No, I don't suppose there is." I stopped to think. "Where does that put finding gold?"

"I expect we'll have to work and suffer for that, too. I never did believe it was sitting around in huge chunks waiting for the picking."

I sighed. "Deep down, I didn't either. The same as I never expected eight-foot-high grass in Oregon."

Finished with the ointment for the moment,

I wiped my hands on my pants and leaned back against a barrel to toy with my short-cropped hair. The mangled clumps brought Mama to mind for the first time since we'd snuck aboard. I certainly hoped she kept to her promise of praying for us every hour of every day. Robbie and I were going to need all the help we could get.

# TWO

*R*obbie and I stood blinking in the first daylight we'd seen for nearly a week. We'd just been hauled from the *Oriental's* hold, and the brigantine's deck was strangely calm beneath our feet.

"Is this San Francisco Bay?" I wondered aloud. "Is *that* San Francisco?"

Our ship had dropped anchor among others in a wide, half-moon-shaped harbor before a barren rock of an island. Across shallow waters stood a hodgepodge of a town not much bigger than Oregon City. Morning mists were still rising from ramshackle buildings clinging to hills while a cool, early October breeze blew strongly at our backs. At least the fresh air smelled good. I managed to capture a few lungfuls before Captain Fallows himself graced us with his presence. He was toting my rifle.

"Here." He tossed it butt end toward me. "By rights I should confiscate it for passage due. I should also let ye swim ashore. But the currents are surprisingly strong, and ye are probably too young to die. Even I was young once. And maybe ye've learned your lesson."

"Sir!" Robbie snapped to attention, only to wince as the soft flannel of his shirt pulled against his healing back. "We thank you for the lesson, and appreciate the ride ashore."

"Get on with ye, then, before I change my mind!"

Captain Fallows pulled decisively at his cap and stomped off, leaving Robbie and me to follow the last of the passengers down a rope ladder to a waiting dinghy. I went first, Papa's rifle tucked securely once more in the holster I'd made for it on the side of my pack. Robbie tossed me his own pack and followed.

Every one of the half-dozen men on that little boat was silent as we approached the dock. They were all probably thinking the same thoughts as Robbie and I—What do we do first? . . . How do we get to the gold fields just as fast as possible? . . . Will there be any gold left when we arrive? I was also thinking something different from the others. How was I going to get Robbie to the gold fields when he couldn't even carry his pack?

Fresh off the boat, our fellow passengers gave a sudden roar and scattered. We two stood wobbling on our sea legs, staring at the almost deserted streets. Robbie finally cleared his throat to speak.

"Where is everybody, Phoebe?"

"The gold fields. Where else? And if they're up near the mountains, we'd best get there soon, too. Before the winter. Those *Oregon Intelligencer* articles never gave any advice about panning for gold in snow."

Reality hit hard when we entered a mercantile store along Front Street, bordering the harbor. There was a big hand-lettered sign posted by the counter, right next to a little gold-weighing scale: *NO CREDIT!! Gold fixed at $16 the ounce. Don't go off to the fields without your pan, pick, and shovel!*

Robbie and I dropped our packs to explore the goods. When we saw the prices, we both let out loud whistles.

"We don't strike it big, fast, we're going to starve for sure, Robbie."

"At such rates, only the shopkeepers are going to get rich!" He bent to study a wooden box about three feet long labeled "gold-washing rocker." "I heard tell of these, Phoebe. You shovel dirt into the hopper up here, pour water over it, then rock it like a cradle with this handle. The gold should end up on the bottom. It makes the finding much easier."

"Easier or not, it's a hundred and fifty dollars, Robbie."

"I can see that clear as day. And I've only got a hundred and eighty all told." He studied the rocker more closely, then pulled a pencil stub and scrap of paper from his pocket.

"What're you doing?"

"Sketching it. I'll build us one when we arrive. It looks dead easy, and I've a few tools in my pack." He grimaced. "Another reason it's so heavy."

We finally left that store with two pans, a pick and shovel, a heavy loaf of bread, and a couple pounds of bacon. It was all we could afford and still have fares for the launch that was the only way to Sutter's Fort, the gathering point for the gold fields beyond. Luckily, we learned about the launch and its price from the men who'd been going on about it in the store.

We trailed a few of those men to where the launch was docked. It was the least prepossessing boat I'd ever seen: one flimsy mast tottered from the center deck, and paint was peeling everywhere. It was loaded to the gunwales with supplies and already floated low in the water. The would-be miners crawling all over those barrels and bales of supplies didn't help, either. A memory of the roomy, dark hold of the *Oriental* washed over me with unexpected nostalgia.

Robbie purchased tickets for us anyway with

the last of his money. What those tickets bought were rocky seats atop two unclaimed barrels. We stowed our outfit by our feet and settled in as a soggy afternoon fog enveloped us.

"Just a hundred miles or so, Feeb," Robbie said. "Then another forty-five to trek past Sutter's Fort to where the first gold was found. We can survive it."

The launch pushed off.

We dined on bread and slabs of uncooked bacon for five days until bacon and bread both gave out. Meanwhile, the launch sailed us across a dank San Francisco Bay to ride the tide through a narrow strait. Six hefty men rowed us past the mosquito-infested Sacramento Delta, then on up the Sacramento River.

It was dry and hot by Sutter's Fort, and that cheered us, even famished as we were. Maybe it was the fact of finally arriving that buoyed us, too. Actually climbing off that perfidious launch and walking the three short miles from the river to the solid, white adobe walls of the famous Mr. Sutter's domain. But our true change in fortune began when we nearly stumbled over a body sprawled flat on its stomach in the dirt in front of one of the grogshops that seemed to be filling the open cubicles inside John Sutter's fort.

Robbie had been sort of half dragging his pack, and let go of it and the shovel both. I dropped the heavy pick and slipped my own pack off to bend over the figure.

"Is he breathing, Feeb?" Now that we were exclusively surrounded by men, Robbie was calling me this on a regular basis. I was grateful that he hadn't taken advantage of that Francis Benedict.

I prodded at a shoulder, and the man flopped over on his back. He let out a vast snore, laced over- whelmingly with what I strongly suspected was the Demon Rum. "Blind drunk, Robbie. And just lying here so peaceful. Should we try and wake him?"

"I don't know. If that's what he wants to be doing—"

A bunch of villainous-looking miners staggering past just then shot our man a glance. They halted as one and began prodding at each other, pointing at something. My eyes followed their fingers to a bulging leather bag attached to the intoxicated man's belt. *Gold.* It had to be. And I didn't care for the covetous expressions on those red-eyed, un- shaven faces. Not one bit. I began shoving at the man.

"Come on, sir! Wake up! Before all your gold's stolen from you!"

"*Mmph* . . . What? Who's calling? What dulcet tones do my ears detect?"

I lowered my voice as gruffly as I could. "It'll be the angels themselves, you don't wake up soon!"

The inebriated gentleman swayed first to a sitting position, blearily caught sight of the hovering vultures, and managed to pull himself upright.

He was a sight. He seemed to be wearing every stitch of clothing he owned, despite the heat. A long, dust-encrusted black coat slid down his skinny body. It covered three waistcoats that I could count, four shirts, and the edge of some nearly black long underwear. High boots with holey woolen stockings poking out of them completed the lowermost part of the picture.

Perhaps he was less drunk than I thought. As my head rose from assessing his footgear, I caught him fiddling with his hands to conjure from nowhere an impressively long, sharp-edged dagger. He flourished its gleaming blade in the direction of the lurking miners as if it were a sword.

"Avast, ye scoundrels! Away! Or be perforated in ten separate locations!"

The mangy bunch disappeared into the nearest rum hole with dispatch. Robbie and I traded glances. Robbie's mouth still hung open at the apparition before us, and I wasn't sure what to make of it, either.

Squinting through the midday sun, this amazing gentleman made the knife disappear. Next he removed a tall beaver hat, revealing a tasseled nightcap beneath. When doffed, underneath that nightcap was nothing but a head as smooth and hairless as an egg. It was a thin, slightly pointy egg opposed by an equally smooth, pointy chin and ears that stuck out at two different angles. The lot was finished off by a surprisingly straight, firm nose. This visage would have been a nightmare but for the only signs of hair upon it: two darkly black eyebrows curved in permanent question marks above red-rimmed eyes and a kind smile.

The rest of this curious person nearly returned to the dust with his doffed cap. I ran to give him a supporting arm. He was grateful.

"Jonathan Overbeam at your service, young man. At your service, distinctly. You seem to have saved my bacon."

"My pleasure entirely, sir." Mr. Overbeam swayed on my arm. "They wouldn't have any coffee hereabouts, would they?" I asked.

"Indeed, they would. Would you care for a cup? Better yet, why not let me treat you and your giant of a friend to a small tot—"

"No tots for us, sir. And definitely no more for you. There's trouble in that!"

He clapped the nightcap back upon his head with a wince. The beaver hat followed, awry. It was a relief to see his noggin protected again.

"You are exceptionally bright for such a stripling. Come. Let us pursue the coffee. Let us also pursue my faithful Indian companion, Olimpio. I fear he has fallen by the wayside, felled by life's temptations as well."

At the mention of an Indian, Robbie had popped his head into the nearest cubicle and now reported back. "Has he got long hair, buckskin trousers, and nothing else? If so, he's inside sleeping in a pool of whiskey."

Jonathan Overbeam peered up at Robbie. "Fetch him, like a good giant. And conduct him to the modest eating establishment across the court."

Robbie took off on his errand, and I reached for our packs and tools and dragged them in a trail of dust across the courtyard. Soon we were all present, watching Mr. Overbeam place an order with a slovenly man in a stained white apron.

"Coffee for the four of us." He considered Robbie and me blearily. "No food for myself or my faithful companion, but I suspect these two would like the works."

Would we ever! My mouth was already watering in anticipation before Robbie almost squelched the deal.

"Sir—" Honest as ever, he reached out thick fingers to touch Jonathan Overbeam's shoulder. "We've only just arrived. We've no money to pay."

The gentleman waved a skinny hand barely hanging on to a skeletal wrist. "It matters not a whit. My treat, lad. My treat."

Saved! Shortly Robbie and I were tucking into the best meal we'd eaten in weeks. Bowls of thick stew and fresh, thick bread to go with it. It wasn't fancy, but there was lots of it. There was even butter for the bread. We ate ravenously—so ravenously that it wasn't until I couldn't eat another bite that I finally noticed Mr. Overbeam staring at me. Several cups of coffee had improved his bearing remarkably, and his eyes were clearer and shrewder than I would have expected. He hacked something from his throat and shot it expertly through the open door nearby. Then he lowered his head conspiratorially and beckoned us close.

I hunched forward over the plank table and Robbie, after a final swallow, followed. The Indian Olimpio was still glazed and ignored us all. Mr. Overbeam commenced.

"Recent experience leads me to believe that

Olimpio, whilst truly a constant friend, and a great seer amongst his tribe, to boot—" Overbeam's head clonked into mine, then shot back. "Recent experience, of which you two partook so nobly, leads me to believe that I might need some managing."

This was a secret? I eased my overfull stomach away from the hard edge of the table as Jonathan Overbeam continued.

"Although currently a man of means, and having the means to become an even greater man of means—" He giggled. "I am fond of words. My only weakness, aside from the obvious." His head bobbed upright. "To simplify a complex story . . . might you two be interested in joining forces with me?"

"In what capacity exactly, Mr. Overbeam?" He was an interesting specimen, to be sure, but Papa had never raised me to be gulled.

"I see honesty and strength in the two of you. Compassion and common sense, as well. All virtues somewhat lacking in these environs. You could've walked off with my little bag just as easy as save me." He paused to chuckle. "But then you'd never know where it came from, would you?"

Robbie's eyes were wide as he began to piece things together. "No, sir. But we've come to find our gold honest. Not by the sweat of any other man."

"Oh, you'll sweat enough, for sure. And freeze a little, too. But having a specific direction never hurts." He nodded at the dozing Indian. "And Olimpio's my direction. He's a Digger by birth and nature—a Yalesumni from the Sierras, from gold country. But his tribe's never wanted more than the roots beneath their feet to eat. Gold—bright and yellow, hard and cold—means nothing to him. It does not adulterate the purity of his soul."

As the Indian let out a snore I did wonder briefly why he'd teamed up with this curious man. Why he was consorting with the enemy, so to speak, who was after his birthright. But it wasn't my place to ask, so I didn't.

Meanwhile, Overbeam reached for his coffee and took another swallow. "Help me fetch the supplies, do a little cooking and laundry for me—" He was staring directly at me now, as if he knew my secret. "And you'll be welcome back at my camp."

"Where exactly is your camp, Mr. Overbeam?"

Overbeam glared at Robbie. "That's not a polite question to ask in these parts, young man."

"Sorry, sir," Robbie quickly apologized. "We're brand-new here, remember. We don't know the ways yet."

"You'll learn. It's about an eighty-mile journey

from here. For the moment, that is all you need to know. Are you game?"

Robbie and I caught each other's eyes. We had no idea where to begin now that we'd arrived at the very heart of our quest. We didn't even know how to use our fine new pans and tools—or for that matter, how to tell real gold from false. We'd have to take Jonathan Overbeam on faith—at least for a while.

"Yes, sir!"

"We'll do it!"

Our first chore was to help Mr. Overbeam stock up on several months' worth of provisions for the four of us at the store within the fort. My natural inclination was to go for lots of beans and flour. Although these commodities were not cheap, they were the cheapest foods available. Mr. Overbeam stopped me after I'd had Robbie haul fifty-pound sacks of each into a pile and was directing him after more.

"Allow your mind to soar a little higher, young man."

"You mean we can go for a side of bacon, too? And a jug of molasses?"

"By all means." Overbeam nodded approval to the clerk. Then he took over. "And we'll have two dozen of those tins of sardines, six bottles of lime juice—"

"Those sardines are sixteen dollars the tin!" I wailed. "And the lime juice five each!"

"Scurvy, lad. We must guard against scurvy. And since you point out the prices, I believe we shall also have a half dozen of those brandy bottles. Surely they are a bargain at only eight dollars per."

"Mr. Overbeam, I don't think that's such a good—"

"Enough. The brandy can be medicinal as well. Add a case of those peaches, my good man. And rice. And a sack each of potatoes and onions."

Robbie was behind me, adding it all up in his head. "If my pa could get three dollars the pound for the potatoes and onions he's been growing, I'd never have needed to leave Pudding Creek!"

The final pile of Mr. Overbeam's essentials was horrifying. It didn't seem to bother him a bit, though. He marched right up to the counter with his gold bag. He emptied part of it on a brass tray and waited for the weighing up.

I crept closer, fascinated. I'd never seen real gold before. It was shiny bright, sure enough. Mr. Overbeam's variety was half a sort of golden dust, half little misshapen nuggets. "The size of dried peas, they are," I whispered aloud.

Mr. Overbeam clutched dramatically at his throat. "How could I have forgotten? A tragedy, it might have been! Add twenty-five pounds of dried peas, my good man. I do enjoy a good pea soup."

I shut my mouth. Even with all that gold shining before me, I still couldn't believe our benefactor could afford the supplies he'd amassed.

Outside the shop Mr. Overbeam stood waiting for Robbie and Olimpio and me to lug the stuff to him. He finally noticed Robbie sweating and flinching.

"What ails you, my dear giant? Was I wrong in estimating your capacities for physical labor?"

"No, sir," I shot out protectively. "Not at all. Robbie will be in fine fettle in only a few more days. Strong as a bull he is, usually."

Mr. Overbeam eyed me. "Indeed. And what, then, might be wrong with him at this moment?"

There wasn't anything to do but drag Robbie over and allow Mr. Overbeam a peek at his back. It elicited raised eyebrows, followed by a new flurry of activity. Olimpio was left on guard duty by the pile while Robbie and I were hauled unceremoniously outside the gates of the fort to where a group of tents had been raised. Mr. Overbeam parted the flaps on one and I met my first Celestial.

"Mr. Chin is newly arrived from the Orient," Overbeam explained. "It's my understanding he has some knowledge of medicine."

Mr. Chin inclined his pigtailed head and nodded Robbie inside.

Mr. Overbeam's final purchase of the day was two burros. We overloaded them almost as badly as that Sacramento launch and set forth. The poor creatures traversed a goodly distance from Sutter's Fort, following well-grooved tracks along the American River on the way to Sutter's Mill, before they began to tire. Our little party mostly kept in step. Robbie was walking taller and not wincing as much.

I gave my burro a good tug as it slowed. "Gee, Romeo!"

"I don't think burros take to oxen orders, Feeb."

"I can't help it if that's all I know. What do they listen to?"

Robbie swatted a dusty rump and the creature commenced to move. "Authority."

"If you say so. By the by, I am glad to see you acting so improved. What exactly did Mr. Chin do to you, Robbie?"

"He said the welts were sick, Feeb. He dusted them with something that looked like gunpowder.

He brought a candle close . . . then I don't re-member anything until I woke up. But it truly seems much better, even if it does sting a little. And he gave me a pot of something for you to rub on my back mornings and nights. . . ." Robbie paused, and it almost looked as if he were blushing beneath his several-days' growth of pale whiskers. "Different from that black grease on the ship," he rushed on. "It smells more like herbs and things."

"Fair enough." I ignored his sudden discomfi-ture now that he was no longer feeling at death's door. It was the only way to deal with my necessary nursing services. "As long as it works." I glanced ahead to where Olimpio was leading Juliet, our second burro, and behind to where Mr. Overbeam was strolling as if out for a Sunday walk. "What a curious situation this all is!"

Then I set in to whistling. It was a tune I'd heard for the first time aboard the launch. A catchy thing, it was. The words just took over my head:

> Oh! California, that's the land for me.
> I'm going up the Sacramento with my
> washbowl on my knee. . . .

# THREE

*J*onathan Overbeam's secret diggings turned out to be halfway along the Middle Fork of the American River. It took almost four days to pack in there, each step taking us higher into the foothills, then finally into the wild heights of the Sierra Nevadas themselves. The camp and Mr. Overbeam's strike were along Blackwater Creek, which rushed swiftly through a rocky little valley before joining the Middle Fork.

"There it is!" Mr. Overbeam and Olimpio had paused with the burros atop a ridge overlooking an almost hidden ravine. I glanced below and shuddered at the last of the winding, precipitous trails we'd have to work our way down.

"You've still got plenty of water in your creek," Robbie observed from nearby. "Not like some of the dried-out workings we've passed."

Olimpio grunted. We'd learned in the past few days that he was a man of as few words as Mr. Overbeam was of many. Maybe that's why they got on so well together.

"End of summer, dry time. Soon much rain come. Snow follows."

A shiver traversed my spine. *Snow. Winter.* To winter here might be worse than when the Petticoat Party—my family's westering wagon train—had been almost stranded in the Cascades just short of the Barlow Pass and Oregon City two years back. And hadn't the Sierra Nevadas been the very mountains where the Donner Party met its doom? My eyes drifted across the tight, fir-studded valley. A little snow and we'd be stuck for sure. That's when I made out what seemed to be a roof. At least there was a small stone chimney, poking crookedly between trees to this side of the creek. It was a welcome respite from my cold thoughts.

"You've got a cabin? You never mentioned anything about a having a proper cabin, Mr. Overbeam!"

"As to how proper it is, I will let you make an evaluation, my dear Feeb. But it is a cabin. I paid five hundred dollars for it—my first earnings—from the gentleman who formerly resided here."

"What happened to him?"

"Butterman? He was one of those Mormons who started out digging by Sutter's Mill. There were a group of them working on the sawmill construction before the first strike was discovered. Odd people they were. Gold or no, when they got a

call from Brigham Young to come home to Salt
Lake City, they all packed up and left." Overbeam
fanned himself with his top hat, then moved
toward the narrow trail. "But that is an irrele-
vancy." He swept his hat before him. "As for now,
I cordially invite you to *my* home. Welcome to *El
Dorado!*"

Mr. Butterman had been a fine carpenter. The
log cabin was smaller than my own family's back
in Oregon Territory, but it was tight and snug.
That's where its good points ended. As I threw
open three sets of shutters to let in late afternoon
light, I could see right off why Mr. Overbeam had
suggested he needed some managing. Papa's pigsty
back home was a whole lot cleaner than the innards
of this place. Mr. Overbeam and Olimpio were still
fussing with the burros, but Robbie had walked in
behind me.

"Tarnation, Phoebe!" He was stunned wordless
for a few moments.

"My sentiments exactly, Robbie. I don't even
know where to start. But if you think for a moment
that just because I'm a girl I'm going to spend all
my time setting this to rights, instead of learning
how to pan for gold, you've got another thought
coming!"

"I never said anything about that, Phoebe. Not a word. But we did make an agreement with Mr. Overbeam to—" He lowered his head to back out the door. "Uh, I think I'll just sleep outside tonight, Feeb. Deal with this in the morning—"

"You're evading your responsibilities, Robbie!"

But he was already loping down toward that creek, and in a moment he was bent over it, scooping up a handful of bottom gravel. In the meantime Olimpio was coming toward me, a fifty-pound sack of potatoes slung over one naked shoulder. I was beginning to see red. "Drop that outside the door, Olimpio! The lot of it!"

Surprised, he obliged me. "Why, young Feeb?"

"Because I've got to flush out the Augean stables first, is why!"

Twenty feet away, Mr. Overbeam's mismatched ears perked up. "Bless me! A student of the classics in my midst! And however did you come upon the tale of Hercules, young Feeb?"

"They've got culture in Massachusetts, and they've got both culture and Miss Simpson the schoolteacher in Oregon City, Mr. Overbeam. What they haven't got is a disaster anywhere near to this."

Mr. Overbeam's smile stretched from ear to ear. "I knew I'd chosen properly! It was fate itself that struck me lying in the dust that day at Sutter's Fort!"

I scowled mightily. Stuck. I was stuck with the domestic chores I'd hated all my life. Well, the sooner done, the sooner I could move on to the creek. I hunted for something to use as a broom. There wasn't anything approximating such a tool. Of course there wasn't. I did find an ax, though, while tripping over a three-foot mound of empty tin cans. I hefted the ax and headed for the nearest low-slung fir. Fuming to myself every second, I shortly had a workable broom in hand. Back at the cabin door I turned to glower down toward the creek. Olimpio was already giving Robbie lessons, that was clear. Robbie was swirling his pan in circles, dribbling out bits of gravel and sand.

"Some gold rush!"

I stomped into the cabin and began to sweep.

We all slept under the stars that night. In the morning I cajoled Mr. Overbeam into stripping off a good half of his layers. He did it grudgingly.

"Don't you feel the nip in the air, young Feeb? I'll catch my death of cold, or the ague, or—"

"Stop fussing, Mr. Overbeam. You're the one who asked for laundry service. And the way that sun is heating up, it'll be ninety degrees again soon."

He handed me his third vest and stopped.

"One of those shirts, please, Mr. Overbeam."

"No! I couldn't possibly—"

"Just one of the shirts, Mr. Overbeam. You've got to get accustomed to the idea. Tomorrow I'm having the rest."

His skinny arms hugged his emaciated body protectively. "Never! I'm *never* out of the last three layers, and my underwear!"

"That's fairly obvious, but you will be tomorrow, Mr. Overbeam. I assure you, you will be."

Overbeam made a supplicating gesture toward Robbie. "Help me! Young Feeb's gone out of control!"

Robbie laughed. "You set the terms, Mr. Overbeam. You even bought laundry soap back at Sutter's Fort. Feeb intends to complete those terms of our contract as fast as possible, and move on to the gold."

"I take it all back, young Feeb! Find your gold!"

"Too late," I spit out. "For you, too, Robbie. Before any of you starts panning today, I want a hole dug a good distance from the cabin. A big hole. You and Olimpio better get busy. 'Cause when it's done, you're both responsible for carting off all the garbage and stowing it in that hole."

"But . . . but . . . Feeb—"

"No buts about it. After that, I want another hole dug for a latrine. The lot of us live like pigs, we're going to be sick before the rains, lime juice and brandy in stock or not!"

I turned away to allow Mr. Overbeam to peel off his shirt in privacy. I couldn't see him shake his head, but I knew he was doing it.

"A monster," he mourned. "I've brought a veritable monster into our midst."

I didn't bother to reply, but I knew Mama would be proud of me.

I was saddled indefinitely with the domestic work. It wasn't because Mr. Overbeam suspicioned my true gender, though. Rather, the fault lay in the fact that I was physically the smallest and least strong of our little household. Robbie's and Olimpio's brawn were needed for the mining. Even emaciated Mr. Overbeam turned out a lot tougher and more sinewy than his appearance let on. Perhaps it was for the best. At least I knew that if I cooked, I needn't fear spoiled food. Resignation did little to improve my frame of mind over the business, however.

Three hot and hot-tempered days later, the El Dorado situation was shipshape and under control—at least to my basic specifications. The afternoon of the third day I tidied up the tin dishes and cups from our communal dinner and set a caldron of pea soup to simmer over the fire. Before heading for the creek at last, I gave my new domain one final inspection.

The open door and two glassless windows that faced the water let in enough light to admire the plank floor I'd scrubbed smooth and clean with creek sand. Rough but sturdy shelving to either side of the fireplace held our cooking and eating implements, as well as the tinned foods, neatly stacked next to a few feet of Mr. Overbeam's books. Under the single window on the far wall the former owner had built wooden bins that now held our sacked provisions. A central plank table and benches filled in most of the remaining floor space, aside from Mr. Overbeam's bed, which was built into the far corner the way Mama and Papa's was at home. Papa's rifle held the place of honor on the mantel-shelf, and over the open rafters above my head I'd neatly slung our aired blankets out of the way till nightfall. I nodded to myself in satisfaction at the general orderliness and finally made it out the door.

Robbie had taken yesterday off to build a gold-washing rocker from his sketches, and now he and Olimpio were fussing with it. Mr. Overbeam was off somewhere in the nearby rocks, poking around with his pick in search of the Mother Lode.

I stood under the protective foliage of a creek-side tree for a few minutes, just taking in the scene. The Blackwater was maybe thirty feet across—wider than some rivers I'd forded along the Oregon Trail. It was shallow, like the Platte, but that was the only similarity between the two. The waters in this creek were almost black and ran fast over out-croppings of water-smoothed, rounded boulders. Even with all its eager energy, I could see it was not at the height of its powers. Flood marks from former seasons showed how high the creek could go when the rains came. It would overflow its banks, for a surety, and probably flood nearly to the front door of the cabin.

My attention shifted to Robbie and the Indian. They were both bare-backed now. Robbie was bent over his machine, and I could see perspiration pooling around his healing scars. The results of that flogging hardly bothered him anymore, but he'd have livid welts for the rest of his life. I already knew those scars better than the back of my hand. I could map their wanderings in my sleep, and often did, waking up sweaty and confused. For the first time in ages I remembered the Sioux blood-sister mark on my palm. Now we both had scars, Robbie and I.

"Hey, Feeb!" Robbie noticed me with a delighted grin. "This rocker really works. Look, only a couple of hours we've been using it, and I'll bet we've found upwards of three ounces of gold!"

I walked over. "Let me see."

Robbie pointed to his pan nearby, where a fine sand of gold gleamed brightly.

"Not bad, Robbie. That'll pay for three tins of sardines."

"*Here*, Feeb. In California. But not in Oregon."

Olimpio grunted and leaned back on his bare heels. "Too slow. You want much gold, must dig in rocks. Find where sand comes from."

"You mean it's not been sitting in this creek forever?" I asked.

Robbie shoved damp, sun-streaked hair from his eyes and answered my question. "Olimpio's been explaining the whole business for me. What we're dredging out is only the bits and pieces the weather washes down from the rocks in the mountains. We need to find what Mr. Overbeam is searching for—a thick, natural vein in the rocks themselves."

I studied the jagged cliffs surrounding us. "A little like searching for a needle in a haystack, that'd be."

"Right. That's why most of the miners just go

for the wash-off. They can meet their expenses and maybe stash a little away."

I was dubious about that. "If they're lucky. In the meantime somebody show me how to handle one of these pans."

"Roll up your trousers, Feeb. You've got to stand in the river for that."

I pulled off my boots and socks, rolled up Papa's trousers even more, and took the plunge.

"Yow!"

I jumped back out again. "It's cold! Freezing cold!"

Robbie snickered. "You're learning. The water's mostly from melted snow. Another reason the rocker is useful. We don't have to stand in the creek all day. Why don't you just haul buckets of water for the rocker?" He nodded toward the canvas pail by the stream's edge. "It'll go faster."

"Not before I get the hang of using the pan." I was adamant. "I've come to pan for gold, and darned if I'm going home without learning how." I plunged back into the icy stream.

A few hours in the Blackwater Creek had me sweating above the waist, and turning blue beneath. It also bequeathed me sore arms and the very devil of a backache. I persevered, however.

Tip the lip of the pan into the creek gravel for a full load. Swish the lot around till water and sand both wash off. Add more water to the remains and repeat the process about fifteen times. Gold was heavier than anything else. If there was any sitting in your pan, it would eventually be the last thing remaining.

I sloshed through the rapid currents of that stream for a long time, scaring tiny minnows and frogs sunning on rocks, seeking my first gold. Colorful butterflies floating at nose level and delicate water bugs skittering across occasional boulder-bound pools became nothing but inconveniences to be waved off. When it finally came, I couldn't believe it.

"Gold! I found gold!"

Aching back forgotten, I splashed to shore to properly exhibit my find. "It's not any piddling little grains, either!"

Robbie and Olimpio both peered into my pan.

"Son of a gun, Feeb. You've found a nugget!"

I had. A lovely nugget twisted into the shape of a groundnut. It was almost as big as one, too. Robbie dropped the handle of the rocker he'd been turning.

"Whereabouts did you find it, Feeb? Maybe there's more."

Robbie and Olimpio followed me into the cold creek. There was more. Olimpio studied the smaller nuggets that washed out in his pan, then he turned to the rocky slope directly edging the far side of the shore. "Up there." He pointed. "Get picks."

When Mr. Overbeam returned empty-handed from his own prospecting search, he found us scrambling halfway up the face of the ravine on the opposite shore from the cabin, struggling for footholds while we poked into crevices. He joined us, drove his pick once into the closest piece of rock, and let out a yell.

*"Eureka!"*

"What's that?" Robbie asked.

"Eureka! I've found it! We've found it! The Mother of all Mother Lodes!"

Was it possible? "Just like that?" I edged over to peek.

"*Not* just like that, young Feeb. I protest. With vehemence. Olimpio and I have been struggling lo these many—"

For once I ignored the continuing spate of words. Beneath Mr. Overbeam's pick was a strip of gold as thick as my wrist, running straight through and into the center of the rock, into the center of the mountainside. With a finality as sudden as the discovery, the sun fell behind the mountains and shadows overtook us. The glint of the gold died as quickly.

"Tarnation! I've forgotten the pea soup!" I grabbed a pick and slid down the mountain to the creek's edge, then waded across to the cabin.

# FOUR

*M*r. Overbeam was not enjoying his pea soup to the extent I had anticipated that night. As a concession to the new gentility of the cabin, he'd removed his top hat before sitting at the table. But the tassel of his ever-present nightcap jerked hither and yon about his skinny neck as he erratically maneuvered a spoonful of the soup halfway to his mouth, lowered it, then tried again. He finally abandoned the spoon in his bowl.

"I fear the events of the day have overcome my appetite. My sincerest apologies, young Feeb, but I believe a touch of the brandy is called for. It might settle my quaking innards."

"Nonsense," I replied. "What you really need is to tell us what you intend to do with all that gold you found."

"Do. *Do?* Why, for starters . . ." He stopped. "I truly don't know. An event of this magnitude . . . the *quest* has always been all for me. My entire life . . ."

Jonathan Overbeam was suddenly speechless. I took pity on him, he was that forlorn. "Find the brandy, Robbie, and measure out a small allotment for Mr. Overbeam. None for Olimpio, though. The rest of us have to keep our wits about us."

Olimpio, across from me and leaning into the table next to Mr. Overbeam, seemed about to protest. He emitted a snort.

"Feeb talk like squaw."

Strained silence reigned as the Indian returned to his soup. Olimpio did have a point. I'd have to watch that the housework didn't completely un-man me, so to speak. At last the moment passed, and Robbie rose to fetch the brandy.

The first sip seemed to settle Mr. Overbeam. He rediscovered his voice. It wandered rich and full around the edges of the flickering flame of the single candle illuminating the table. But his words had nothing to do with the topic at hand. Or had they?

"I've had something of a checkered career in my time, dear friends. And I blame it all on love. I was thwarted in love young, very young." He reached for his cup again. "My somewhat bizarre physiognomy was repellent to the poor lass I'd set my cap for. Not that she was a great beauty herself, but her mind—ah her *mind*! I felt sure that with two such strong intellects, accommodations could be made. Alas."

Poor Mr. Overbeam. Who'd have guessed he was once in love? Who'd have guessed he had any notion whatever of what it entailed? "Where did you start out, sir? Where were you born?"

"Why, in Philadelphia, of course. The city of Benjamin Franklin, the city of Brotherly Love, the birthplace of our great nation. But after my offers were spurned, I ran off to sea, hoping to drown my sorrows in the great blue void. Not literally, mind you. I wasn't *that* heartbroken.

"I worked merchant schooners between Philadelphia and the Old World. Whaling never called to me. I couldn't be part of harvesting such lovely great beasts." He drank again, gazing off through the distance of years. "I stayed on in England for a time, seeking truth in the land and literature of my forebears. Yet always there was that gaping hole within my being, the knowledge that I would never be loved for myself—"

He swallowed the remainder of his drink and reached for the brandy bottle. I caught his hand. Squawlike or not, it was necessary.

"I'll not allow you to turn maudlin on us, Mr. Overbeam. Not after the day we've had. And surely the genuine affections of the three of us must be some consolation to you!"

"Of course they are! You are the three most faithful companions a poor wretch like myself could wish for—" His long fingers snaked toward the bottle. I snared it first and pulled it just slightly beyond his grasp. He gathered himself together.

"You are right, young Feeb. 'Wine maketh a man act like an ass in a rich pasture.' Some ancient Arabian philosopher or other said that. Too true it is. One sip and already I begin to lose my perspective." His hand slammed upon the table, rattling the bowls. "Of course I know what to do with all that gold!"

"What?" Robbie asked.

I wanted the answer to that myself. Even Olimpio seemed mildly intrigued.

Overbeam reached for his spoon and this time managed to slurp some soup into his mouth. "Excellent, young Feeb. Just the way I like my pea soup. You do have a way with food."

I waited only long enough for him to swallow another dollop. "So, what *will* you do with the gold? You can't keep us in suspense this way, Mr. Overbeam."

He smiled a beatific smile. "I shall share it four ways, between all of us. Share and share alike. Then

I shan't have to worry about its disposition entirely by myself. You found the original nugget after all, Feeb. Olimpio sniffed out the proper area it came from. And our giant Robbie was sure to pound through the entire side of that mountain sooner or later." He sat back with relief and satisfaction both upon his face.

"Gracious," I breathed. "Imagine the improvements Papa could make on the homestead with all that gold. He could send East for that reaping machine he's been hearing about. We could build a proper house for Mama. With straight-cut planks from Dr. McLoughlin's sawmill."

Robbie's eyes sparkled. "I could set up my own homestead. Get out from under Pa and be my own master."

Olimpio spoke for the second time that evening. "White people keep strange desires. Gold only good to look at. It belongs to mountains. Take too much, spirits become displeased. I sleep now."

True to his word, Olimpio left the table to roll himself in blankets by the fire. That left the three of us to stare at each other. "And what about you, Mr. Overbeam?" I finally asked. "What will you do with your share?"

He cast another longing look toward the brandy bottle, but controlled himself. "I shall select some felicitous town, choose myself an abode, and amass for myself a collection of the great written works of the world. A Gutenberg Bible, perhaps," he mused, "and Shakespeare's First Folio. . . . Then I shall bolt the doors and be done with the rest of humanity forever."

"You mean even Robbie and I won't be allowed to visit?"

"Well, certainly, old and treasured friends—"

Robbie rose from the bench. "This is silliness. All of it. Olimpio's got more sense than any of us. I'm for sleep, too. The vein looks good, but it might be a fluke. In the morning we'll learn just how far it goes—"

"—And how upset the mountain spirits are likely to get," I finished.

We'd set the burros loose to roam at their liberty around the valley on first arriving. In the morning I woke to the sounds of Romeo's and Juliet's neck bells tinkling directly outside our cabin. I pulled myself from my bedroll to observe that everyone else was gone. Robbie's blankets were neatly stacked in a small pile, as was his wont. Mr. Overbeam's raised wooden bed was a jumble of tortured quilts. Olimpio's coverings had been kicked into the nearest corner next to the long row of supply bins. I shook my own blankets and slung them over a rafter, helped myself to the soup still warming by the fire, and was soon squinting from the cabin door into another bright, dry morning.

Across the creek I could make out three figures banging away at the wall of the mountain that hemmed us into our valley. *El Dorado.* The fabled land of riches beyond belief or understanding. Had we really found it? I supposed I should still be excited, but a new day cast new light on things. The proof would be in the pudding, yet questions tugged at my brain. Why would Olimpio still be working at extracting gold when he felt the way he did about it? Why in the world was he working with Mr. Overbeam at all? Mulling over this mystery yet again brought me no closer to an answer, so I left the shelter of the cabin to absently stroke Romeo. I finally hiked up Papa's trousers, shouldered my boots, and waded into the creek to make the crossing.

"Hey, sleepyhead!" Robbie's face was already streaked with dust when it smiled down on me. "We've followed the vein almost a yard, and it's stronger than ever!"

I clambered up the rocks to get a better look at Mr. Overbeam's Mother Lode. "What's all that white stuff around the gold?"

"Quartz, young Feeb," Mr. Overbeam answered. "Our gold is embedded in quartz."

"How are you going to separate one from the other?"

"We'll just hack it out in chunks and worry about that later."

Hack they did, and with a will. There wasn't anywhere near enough room up there for all of us, though, so I ended up ferrying the extracted chunks down the mountain to a growing pile by the creek. About midday, pausing to wipe sweat from my eyes, I noticed something unusual. Romeo and Juliet had started in to braying. They must have wandered behind the cabin, for I couldn't see them anymore, but their dander was definitely up.

"Robbie! Mr. Overbeam?"

"What is it, Feeb?"

"Something's not right. Something—" I lifted my eyes to the far ridge above our valley and quaked. Something was *wrong*. Four men stood there, rifles in hand. My eyes slid along the outlines of our private trail. Another had already begun the descent. Probably more than one. There was probably at least one more behind the cabin, harrying our burros. Six men, at the least. And their intentions did not appear honorable.

Mr. Overbeam was squinting across the creek. He prided himself on his farsightedness. "Bless me. I was well and truly inebriated back at Sutter's Fort, and yet . . . there seems to be a distinct resemblance. . . ."

Olimpio was already sliding down the scree to my level, scattering the loose mass of stones everywhere. In a moment he was tossing the heavily veined chunks from my careful pile into the creek. "Bad men. Hide gold."

I tossed with him until the evidence was gone. The chunks could be found eventually, of course, but if we were indeed about to be robbed, at least we'd give the villains something to work for.

Above Olimpio and me, Robbie and Mr. Overbeam were being just as industrious. Robbie had been banging with a sledgehammer at the overhang above the gold vein. Now I heard a dull rumble. Mr. Overbeam scampered to one side, while Robbie raced before the small avalanche he'd created. In a moment he was next to me, rubble dogging his feet.

"It'll take some doing for them to find that vein now, Feeb."

"I should say so." I watched Mr. Overbeam tentatively pick his way down through the debris. "It'll be a wonder if *we* ever find it again." My complaint was halted right there as one of the intruders appeared before the cabin, rifle pointed. At us.

"Get yerselves across!" he bellowed. "Hands high!"

"We're not unchristian—" The snicker that followed belied the words. "Yer welcome to yer bedrolls, but that's it. No weapons or food. Anger ought to fill yer bellies just fine all the way back to civilization. No pots or gold pans, either. We'll be needing them."

They *were* the men who'd almost robbed Mr. Overbeam back at Sutter's Fort. I recognized them instantly, especially bunched up at close quarters like we were in Mr. Overbeam's cabin. With their rifles still cocked and aimed, staring at them was about all I could do. Aside from jaw a little.

"How'd you find us?"

"Close yer mouth, squirt."

The leader was a man the others referred to as Bog. He was stringy-haired, filthy, and unshaven, and definitely had a mean streak in him longer than Captain Fallows's.

"But since yer *inquire*—" The others smirked at his fancy word, and he scowled those smirks right off their faces. "Yer left a trail a mile wide. It weren't nothin' to follow, were it, boys?"

"No, boss."

"Not atall, Bog."

Bog smiled, revealing chipped, blackened teeth. "There yer have it. The boys and me agree on a bunch of things. One being that we intend to get rich, fast. The other being that we ain't too particular how we do it, long's it don't involve too much *strenuous* labor. Right, boys?"

"In spades, boss."

"You got a way with words, Bog."

Mr. Overbeam had remained strangely mute throughout this entire interchange. He finally summoned up his indignation and courage both.

"This is vastly irregular. This is highway robbery. And highway robbery has no place in this great gold rush. Here in California each man has the liberty to find his own riches, the freedom to keep them. It's an American right!"

"Shut yer trap, ugly-face!" Bog swung his rifle butt at Mr. Overbeam's head. Mr. Overbeam dodged it tidily. "Start packing, afore I change my mind about the Christian part."

I stared at Olimpio, whose face showed no emotion whatsoever. Next, I caught Robbie's eye. His face was easier to read. Across its broad, honest surface flowed outrage, sadness, and resignation in turn. I shrugged at him. "Easy come, easy go."

Bog's rifle butt whacked the back of my legs, hard.

"I told yer not to talk!"

I winced and hobbled over to my blankets.

We'd been escorted to the top of the ridge, then abandoned. In the fading afternoon light the four of us stood staring down at our former domain. All six members of the gang were scurrying around like busy ants. Half were fussing with Robbie's rocker, the other half scrambling up the far mountain face, poking around for our hidden vein.

"Give those skunks a day or two," I sighed, "and that cabin's going to look like Hercules' worst nightmare. And they got Papa's rifle, too. Why should it be so hard to hang on to one rifle?"

"So much for Shakespeare's First Folio," mourned Mr. Overbeam.

"And I'll have to wait on that homestead till I'm a full twenty-one and can claim land legal," Robbie added. "By that time, there won't be any prime land left in the entire Willamette Valley."

Olimpio grunted. We waited for what might be forthcoming.

"Mountain spirits angry now. Chase us away. But spirits learn Bog and company worse. Much worse. We get valley back by and by."

"How, Olimpio? Should we return to Sutter's Fort and report this to the authorities?"

"There are no authorities, young Feeb," Mr. Overbeam informed me. "No police, no sheriff, no judges, no organized justice." It was his turn to sigh. "That was formerly one of the merits of this wild country."

Olimpio smiled for the first time since I'd met him. There was a knowing edge to it, like a fox who's just tricked its pursuers. "Overbeam speaks truth. No good return to Sutter's Fort. No money for white man's things. Time now to live like Indian. Think like Indian." He bent to pull out a viciously sharp knife hidden beneath one buckskin leg, an ax blade from the other. "We have tools. Make weapons. Then valley returns to us."

Mr. Overbeam beamed. "Did I not tell you that our staunch Olimpio is a man in a million? Why return to Sutter's Fort, or even San Francisco? We'd have to rent ourselves out like peons just to get a reasonable stake together again. We'll stay and fight like men for what is ours!"

He reached within his own layers to produce first his own dagger, next a number of items that turned me awestruck in short order. These included two bottles of lime juice, four tins of sardines, a tin of peaches, his little gold-weighing scales, a sadly depleted leather bag usually bulging with gold dust, and an untouched bottle of brandy. "For medicinal purposes." Mr. Overbeam grinned.

"But how in thunder did you. . . . *How?*" Robbie was nearly stuttering.

"I neglected to mention that I spent a few formative years on the Continent, as well. Studying with an itinerant Italian conjuror of some talent." Mr. Overbeam reached beneath the rear folds of his long black coat to produce his ultimate triumph.

"A gold pan!" I exclaimed.

*"Voilà!"* Mr. Overbeam's fingers twitched only slightly, and the one gold pan separated into two. "Cookpot, dining plate, and the means for our financial survival, all intact."

Mr. Overbeam deserved a kiss on his skinny cheek at the least, but I forbore. "You are a wonder!"

"No more so than Olimpio." He turned to the Indian. "Lead on, Macduff. The next move is yours."

# FIVE

We slept under the stars that night, as we had on the first night we arrived at El Dorado. In the morning Olimpio took one look at the sky and spoke.

"Rain comes soon. Need shelter fast."

I studied the same sky. It didn't seem all that different. Maybe a little watery around the edges of the sun. And there were a few more clouds than usual off in the far distance. Come to think of it, those clouds had a different shape to them than the ones we'd been used to seeing—sort of thin and tight, like pancakes without leavening, these were.

"What kind of a shelter, Olimpio?" I asked. "A lean-to?"

"Not strong enough. Bad rains. Find cave."

Olimpio was now definitely in charge. Mr. Overbeam and I were directed to cave finding. Olimpio and Robbie settled in to create working tools from our bits and pieces. When Mr. Overbeam and I returned to the campsite at noon, laid before Robbie and the Indian were a functioning ax, a knife-tipped spear, two bows, and a set of slim arrows. Olimpio glanced up.

"Cave?"

"Not much luck," Mr. Overbeam allowed. "We found one overhang with barely enough space beneath to shelter the four of us."

"Eat," Olimpio ordered. "Search more."

I never expected a tin of sardines to taste like sixteen dollars' worth, but the ones we shared for our dinner did. And the can of peaches tasted like several ounces' worth of gold. I licked the rich syrup from my fingers greedily. That lime-flavored water we drank with it all didn't go down badly, either, although a sprinkling of sugar would've been nice.

"Heavenly," I murmured, lying back on the hard ground. "All we need is a thick elk steak to top it off."

"Many elk here," Olimpio informed me. "Robbie and I hunt tomorrow."

That perked me up considerably. "Why, it'll be just like on the Oregon Trail!"

"Do not know Oregon Trail. But these mountains good. Give respect, they will feed us."

Mr. Overbeam groaned to his feet. "Come along, young Feeb. Shelter is expected of us, and shelter we must find. We can't let our partners show us up this badly."

The two of us headed up another, different piece of mountain this time. We were maybe only a mile or two from El Dorado, but to the north of that hidden valley. It was country other miners had not yet found. It was country perhaps no white person had yet explored. I doggedly climbed flinty scree through thinning trees until I spied something promising.

"Mr. Overbeam?"

"Yes, young Feeb?" He slowly puffed up behind me, red in the face. "The altitude becomes debilitating, Feeb. My feet expand and my lungs contract. Pray make your discovery soon."

"Maybe I have." Before us was a small, sloped mountainside meadow. A natural ring of boulders fenced in the front of it, almost like castle walls. A trickling brook worked its way from farther up the mountain to wind and meander to one side of the meadow. "Look. Fresh water and natural defenses. And I think, I pray—" *Please, Lord,* I murmured in my head, *please let that outcropping be what I think it is!*

Mr. Overbeam was stumbling toward the far side of the meadow and its out-thrust rocks. "Eureka again!" he shrieked. "Our new domicile!"

←《》→

The cave wasn't fancy. But it was dry and jutted into the mountain far enough to give us all space to sleep and then some. There was also room to make a campfire toward its lip, for when the rains truly arrived.

We were settled around a fire before its mouth by nightfall. The smell of the gold pan filled with a simmering mixture of the handfuls of rice and beans I'd secretly stuffed in my blankets gave us all heart. We took turns sipping brook water from our empty peach tin as we waited for the meal. Robbie was in finer fettle than I'd ever seen him.

"Olimpio is fantastic, Feeb! He gave me lessons with the bow and arrows this afternoon. He said I had potential!"

A snort from Olimpio's side of the fire. "Said maybe Robbie manage squirrel, like my baby son."

"You have a son, Olimpio? You have a family?"

"Had all. Sickness took. Medicine man cannot cure. Olimpio search for peace, find Overbeam."

"Oh. Dear." I hadn't really wanted my mystery solved this way.

Mr. Overbeam touched my arm. "Not to fret, young Feeb. Olimpio's family is surely in the Happy Hunting Grounds. Safely away from this vale of tears and mad gold seekers."

"But still—" Tears had already filled my eyes. And only a moment before I'd been so happy, so content. "I do hope my little Sioux brother, Yellow Feather, is safe out on the great prairie. And my mama and papa, and sister Amelia back in Oregon Territory . . ."

Robbie let out a large snuffle. "Ain't thought about the youngsters back home in ages. It'll be colder in Oregon right now. Maybe they've already gotten their first snow."

Mr. Overbeam cleared his throat. "Homesickness is not permitted in El Dorado Two. Strictly *verboten*. How about that supper, Feeb? Surely the rice is ready by now?"

"The supper?" I poked at it halfheartedly with a stick. "I suppose so. Light that torch you made, Robbie, so I can see to serve."

Robbie lit the torch, then leaned back into the cave with it a moment to reach for something. "Hey— Feeb! Olimpio! Mr. Overbeam! Look at this!"

I dropped the cooking stick. "What is it? More gold?"

"Nope. Something way more interesting."

Supper forgotten, we crowded inside to study the cave interior. The afternoon light hadn't been right for it, but now with the flaming torch we could see the roughly arched ceiling. It was covered with pictures. Hand-painted pictures. "Skinny little people," I whispered. "And animals."

Mr. Overbeam pointed at a concentric ring of bold red circles. "Surely that must signify the sun. And there's the moon above, in all its phases!"

For once Olimpio spoke without the grunt. "Is good. Is old sacred place. Very old. Very sacred. We be safe here. Protected by the spirits."

That was a relief. We all slept well that night after a good supper.

The sky was completely overcast the next morning. Olimpio bolted his breakfast of rice and beans and snatched up his bow.

"Robbie, come. Find elk before tracks wash away with rain."

The two hunters disappeared, leaving Mr. Overbeam and myself to manage the domestic chores. I made another fir broom and tidied up our abode. Mr. Overbeam collected rocks to construct a circular fireplace within the cave. Together we gathered great piles of wood and tinder to store inside its dryness. Finally, I fashioned mattresses and fireside seats from soft fir boughs, just as I had for that other cave, that snow cave back in the Cascades so long ago.

For all I was dressed like a boy and made every attempt to act like a boy—right down to copying Robbie's long strides and even making an occasional foray into spitting—I certainly seemed to be ending up with more housework than I'd done back on the homestead. I finally complained about it to Mr. Overbeam. Not complained exactly, but just sort of pointed out the fact that I might've liked to try those bows and arrows, too.

"We can't all have the glory roles, young Feeb," he replied. "Some of Shakespeare's most provocative characters are mostly used offstage. Take Rosencrantz and Guildenstern, for example—"

"You may take them, Mr. Overbeam, as I have no idea who they might be. But it does seem I've spent an awful amount of time cleaning and making up beds lately."

He gave me a shrewd glance. "Well, then, consider the role of the cabin boy on a sailing ship. He might deem himself lowly, but he's the one who keeps everything well greased—keeps the captain happy, and therefore the crew. Cabin boys have been known to grow into captains themselves."

"If you say so, Mr. Overbeam."

Somewhat mollified, I proceeded with my duties. The day passed. And with the evening came Robbie and Olimpio dragging a mighty elk.

Robbie dropped his side of the antlers to arch his back and rub at his arms. "Tarnation, but that takes it out of a man. We've got to make some kind of ropes for the next time."

"What a beauty!" I was all prepared to properly fuss over the victorious hunters, but apparently it was unnecessary. Olimpio already had his knife at work on our dinner. In minutes he had the skin expertly stripped from the carcass. "Feeb. Clean skin. Will have many uses."

Olimpio's order to the lowly cabin boy and camp domestic didn't even rile me. Not on this subject. "You don't have to tell me how, Olimpio. This will be my second elk skin!"

His eyes found mine briefly, just to make sure I was speaking truly. "Good." He handed me the liver. "Cook first for supper. Will give much strength. Overbeam"—the orders continued—"build second fire to smoke meat strips."

We worked long into the night so as not to have any of that bounty wasted. No one complained about the hours, or doing chores beneath them. Everyone had a role, and each was needed. Working together like that, for a reason—our mutual survival—took me back to the early days of the Petticoat Party. Right back to when Miss Simpson had assumed leadership after our men had been mostly done in by that buffalo massacre.

The rest of that trip along the Oregon Trail had been run by women. Strange, but it only now occurred to me that the parts had been reversed here in California. Back on the trail I'd been a girl learning to do a man's job. Here were men trying to do their jobs as well as women's. Of course I was attempting to do a man's job again, but this time I was actually disguised as a male.

For a moment I almost felt like a spy in the enemy camp. I had to step back out of myself to study Robbie and Olimpio and Mr. Overbeam slaving away like they were. Quietly and with great concentration they were steadily working, without the usual chatter a similar collection of women would have made—always with the exception of Mr. Overbeam, who was muttering some famous speech of Hamlet's under his breath. There'd been a time when I actually believed men were useless. Not any longer.

"Feeb. Feeb?"

I shook the thoughts from my head. "What, Robbie?"

He handed me a thick elk steak he'd just stabbed from the fire. "I sprinkled a little salt on it for you, Feeb. I managed to tuck the salt cake into my pocket before Bog got his hands on it!"

He grinned at me as I eased back from my labors to enjoy the welcome break. "Thank you, Robbie." Suddenly I wasn't a spy anymore, but where I belonged, enjoying my comrades.

Sounds of a raging waterfall woke me the next morning, clear back where I was tucked away in my little cave corner. I lifted my head from the fir-bough pillow. The dimmest of light struggled through the entrance. It was a wonder even such illumination as that managed to make it through the water tumbling over the cave's mouth. I turned my head to where Olimpio was sitting cross-legged, staring.

"Rain starts," he said.

That was fairly obvious. I tried to shake the woolliness from my head. "How long will it last?"

"Long time. Maybe one moon. Maybe more. Till snow comes."

Robbie yawned hugely from his blankets a few feet away. "What do we do in the meantime?"

"Plenty," Olimpio answered.

Olimpio hadn't been fooling with that answer. Olimpio never did. Several days passed within the cave as we carefully preserved the remainder of the elk meat and tanned the elk skin with its own brains, just the way I had with Yellow Feather's elk skin on the Oregon Trail—only perhaps a little more expertly this time with Olimpio overseeing the process.

I surely would have liked that skin as an extra blanket for my bed. The nights were becoming cold. But Olimpio had other uses in mind for it. One was as a sewn bag to hold fresh water within the cave. Another was making strips of rawhide that we wove into a tight length of rope. That left just enough for a vest to cover Olimpio's bare chest. After several days the skin was gone, not a scrap wasted.

"We surely could use another elk or two," I commented one morning. "For blankets. And winter coats for all of us."

Olimpio shook his head. He was wearing his vest, and now he wrapped the new rope around his waist in layers. "Today hunt something different."

I stared out into the still-cascading rain. "In this weather? Whatever could we catch?"

"Overbeam's robbers."

"What would we do with them? You wouldn't . . . hurt them? I mean, they certainly weren't very nice, but still . . ."

Mr. Overbeam was already tightening his long coat about himself. There was a gleam in his eyes. "Not physically, young Feeb. Olimpio's tribe has ever been peaceful. Peaceful, yet resourceful."

Olimpio nodded agreement. "But Overbeam stays. Robbie and Feeb come."

"Nonsense! Of course I must join you! You'd never wreak your revenge without me at hand! It's my cabin!"

Olimpio had made up his mind. "Much wet. Overbeam come, Overbeam fall sick. Too thin. No medicine man here."

"But, but—" Mr. Overbeam cast his eyes to the ceiling and tried a final ploy. "You yourself said the spirits would watch over us in this sacred place, Olimpio."

"Spirits not like wet, either. Overbeam stays. Today we look. Think. Maybe not act." He picked up his weapons and stepped into the rain. Robbie and I followed.

Papa's old slouch hat was little defense against the torrential curtains of water falling everywhere. In moments I was soaked to the skin. By the time Olimpio had led us to the ridge above our hidden valley, I knew I was wet clear through to the bone. Robbie didn't look much better. The fact was, he looked downright miserable standing there shivering. In contrast, the water just seemed to glide off Olimpio's vest and skin. He paid it no mind whatsoever. I suppose that was partly because he was busy staring down into the valley. He pointed.

"Smoke comes from chimney. Good now. Bad later."

"Why?"

Olimpio answered with an exasperation not usually evident. "Bad men *inside*. We steal tools now. Hide. Later, need bad men *outside*."

"All right, Olimpio. Anything you say. Let's just make it fast."

Robbie and I shivered and slithered down our old trail behind the Indian. It was hard, because it had become a small rushing stream itself. At the bottom of the valley I gaped in disbelief. Even knowing it was likely to happen hadn't prepared me for the real event.

The contours of Blackwater Creek had changed completely. Our relatively shallow stream had become a raging mountain river. There was no way it could be forded safely now. It had already begun its flooding, too. I laughed.

"What's so funny, Feeb?" Robbie complained.

"There's no possibility Bog and his band will be able to work on our vein of gold, Robbie. Not for the whole winter. Probably not till spring." I studied the Blackwater again. "Or do any panning, either. It's just all too wild."

Robbie stood there considering. "We couldn't have, either, Feeb. Looks like the season's done for sure."

"Maybe we should just give up and head for San Francisco, after all. Maybe even for home."

Olimpio was suddenly beside us. "No go home. You make deal with Overbeam. Keep honor!"

More rain rushed down my back. "Honor sure is uncomfortable sometimes."

The first part of Olimpio's plan centered around our old garbage pit. We'd covered it with logs and branches to keep the flies down. Now the Indian led us directly to it, and before you knew it we were shoving off the logs. I peered inside.

"Funny thing. Looks like there hasn't been a bit of garbage added to our old stuff."

Robbie pushed next to me. "Nope. Never did figure Bog for the tidy type. He probably doesn't even know it's here."

"Good!" Olimpio joined in. "Here we hide tools."

Well, there seemed to be tools scattered everywhere, already beginning to rust with the rain. The villains had just abandoned them all for the comforts of our cabin as soon as the weather turned. We scurried around, gathering picks and shovels as fast as possible, Bog's as well as our own. The weather hid us and our efforts. Eventually, even Robbie's rocker was lowered into that pit. Then we carefully rolled back the logs, and added a few extra layers of boughs and wet leaves to complete the deception. I stood back to contemplate the results.

"Well, that's all fine and good, Olimpio, and it'll keep our tools in better repair till the spring than Bog would've. But I don't see where the revenge comes in."

"Revenge next. If cannot hurt bad men, *can* make miserable." Olimpio motioned us into the trees behind the cabin. The shutters were closed against the weather, and only the constant stream of smoke proved Bog's presence.

"What are you going to do, Olimpio?"

He put his fingers to his lips, signifying silence. Then he unwound the rawhide rope from his waist and carefully tied one end around a big rock. Grasping the other end of the rope between his teeth, the Indian began to scale the outside wall of the cabin. In a few moments he was straddling the chimney, pulling at the rope to haul up the rock, and carefully and firmly sealing the chimney top with it.

Robbie's eyes grew large as understanding slowly dawned. "Is he doing what I think, Phoebe?"

I snickered. "Olimpio's going to smoke those rascals right out into the weather!"

"Well, the least we can do is make some use of the gesture."

"Whatever do you mean, Robbie?"

"I mean this rear window is about your size, Feeb. We open the shutter and I hoist you in—"

"After they're all safely out, of course."

"Naturally. I hoist you in, maybe you could hoist out a few supplies."

"Potatoes." My mouth was already watering. "Onions."

"Maybe another can of those peaches, Feeb."

"Be reasonable, Robbie. Those peaches are long gone. Probably the sardines, too."

"Yes," he sighed. "You're right."

Olimpio's waving arms finally caught our attention. He pointed to the far side of the cabin. Through the downpour we barely heard the cabin door slam outward, and the gagging coughs of Bog and his men.

"It's now or never, Phoebe."

"Let's do it, Robbie!"

I slid through that window slick as an eel. Once inside, I landed almost directly atop pay dirt. *Don't waste any time, Phoebe,* I warned myself. *No hunting for Papa's rifle. Just get the goods out.* I groped half blindly for the closest bin. It didn't matter what was in it. Billowing black smoke attacked my nostrils and a fit of coughing seized me. On top of every-thing else those idiots were burning green wood. Something else, too. There were rancid tobacco fumes mixed in, and the stink of spilled liquor. Bog had been sitting around guzzling Mr. Overbeam's brandy.

Confused by the onslaught of smoke and odors, I turned away from the bins toward the fireplace and took a tentative step in its direction before I tripped on something round and hard. A kettle? I snatched for it.

"You all right, Phoebe?"

Robbie's concern brought me back on target. "Watch out!" I tossed the kettle out the window. Then my hands grabbed again for a sack. The one I found was a good bit lighter than it should've been. That made it easier to get it to the window.

"Robbie!" I called.

"Lower away, Feeb!"

I went for the next bin along the wall. Soon another sack was out the window. I was reaching for a third when I heard hacking through the thin-ning smoke from the environs of the door. It didn't pay to be greedy. I dropped the sack and stepped on it to poke my head from the window.

"They're coming back, Robbie!"

He was already pulling at my arms. There was a bad moment when I heard the distinct sound of a rifle being cocked. By the time its shot rang out, I was on top of Robbie. He dragged himself out from under, grabbed a sack, and ran for the trees.

"Where's the other sack?"

"Olimpio's got it. You fetch the kettle."

In a few minutes we were all together under a heavy fir cover, partway up the mountain. Bog and his men were running in circles around the cabin below, shooting off their firearms, not even bright enough to first unstop the chimney. Olimpio contemplated his bow and arrow as if thinking about adding to the confusion. Apparently he decided against it.

"Come." He hoisted one of the sacks. "We go home."

Robbie hoisted the other. "Funny thing, Feeb. I don't feel the least bit cold anymore. I feel good!"

# SIX

*W*e roasted big fat potatoes in the coals of the fire that night. Atop the fire, bubbling happily in the deep kettle, was pea soup. I'd missed the onion bag but found Mr. Overbeam's dried peas. He was delighted.

"An onion would've sweetened it, young Feeb, but the elk jerky will make up for any lost flavor." He leaned closer to the rising steam and sniffed of it luxuriously. "Ah. Now we can winter in contentment."

I had other thoughts on that subject, but then, my teeth were still chattering as I sat by the fire, wrapped in every last one of my blankets while my only set of clothes dried. It had seemed such a good idea this morning to emulate Mr. Overbeam's layers and wear Papa's extra woolen shirt atop my first one. Returning to the cave soaked completely through proved me wrong. At least the rear of the cave had been dark enough for me to disrobe in relative privacy. Robbie had cooperated, too. He'd kept Olimpio and Mr. Overbeam by the fire, relating our adventure. Gallant as always, he'd remained in his own sopping clothes until he was certain I was safely swathed. Currently the two of us trembled almost in unison across the flames from each other. Mr. Overbeam hungrily poked at one of the potatoes.

"It seems to me it might behoove us to consider a little further strategy regarding El Dorado One. Now that the initial attack has been made."

"We ain't even warmed up yet, Mr. Overbeam," Robbie complained. "Feels like I'll never be warmed up again."

"Oh, but you will, my dear giant. Youth is resilient. We must press on. Before Bog and his friends recover enough to devise their own set of defenses." He paused. "Before they eat up all the remaining food. Six men big as oxen, after all—"

"Well, we can't very well smoke them out again," I opined. "They'd be on to that one."

"And we can't burn down the cabin itself," Mr. Overbeam mused. "That would be counterproductive, to say the least." He turned to Olimpio. "What do you think, my friend?"

"Overbeam speaks truth. Must strike again. Tomorrow."

"Tomorrow!" I yelped. "Why tomorrow?"

"Soon best. Need plan. Olimpio think."

Olimpio thought all during supper. When there wasn't a speck of food left, he belched contentedly and pointed to the ceiling. "Spirits have answers. Give Olimpio plan." He reached for a twig from the tinder pile and nodded us all close, then began sketching into the dust of the cave floor. We watched and learned.

Mr. Overbeam had no intention of missing the action a second time. We discovered that fact the next morning as plans were improved over breakfast.

"I'm going with you."

Olimpio attempted to stare him down. "Rain still falls."

"Well, let it, says I!" With a flourish, Mr. Overbeam produced from a dark nook the object he'd labored over during our absence the previous day.

"What in the world is that?"

"This, my dear Feeb, is an umbrella!"

"Never seen an umbrella like that before," Robbie muttered.

Mr. Overbeam caught the remark. "Of course you haven't, Robbie. This is *Overbeam's Improved Umbrella!*"

We all stared at the contraption. Apparently, Mr. Overbeam had sacrificed one of his four shirts for his invention. That meant he was truly serious. I couldn't say much for the appearance of the thing, though. The body of the shirt was stretched over a frame of slim, stripped fir boughs, the two shirtsleeves sticking out stiffly beyond, front and rear. To this frame he'd somehow attached a harness that looked suspiciously as if it were sewn from the tails of his black coat.

"Clever, eh?" he chortled. "Properly aligned, there'll be no rain dripping down *my* neck, or into my eyes, either. I'm afraid I had to use most of the elk fat for waterproofing, though." He gingerly touched the outer surface of the device, and his long fingers came away thick with grease. "Guaranteed to stop any amount of water short of Noah's Flood."

I glanced at the waterfall still functioning as our cave door. "You certain sure that Flood isn't upon us now? Maybe it's an ark we should be building, instead of worrying about revenge—"

"Nonsense, young Feeb." Mr. Overbeam struggled into his harness with much fluttering of arms. "See? Overbeam's Improved Umbrella requires no handle, allowing total freedom of the limbs for other uses. How's that for advanced engineering, eh?"

The shirtsleeves jutted forth askew, just like Mr.

Overbeam's ears. The end result gave him the appearance of a very skinny, very hungry predatory bird. I clamped my jaws shut to keep from giggling. Across the fire Robbie was struggling mightily with his own opinions. Olimpio gathered his weapons, ignoring the latest signs of daftness among us.

"If Overbeam ready, Overbeam come."

I slapped on my slouch hat, and out we went to brave the elements.

The cabin sat below us in the rain, smoke once more pouring from its chimney. Blackwater Creek had edged another few feet up the slope toward it. I was wet clear through again and rapidly filling with doubts.

"Do you really think the plan will work? It's so *simple*."

Mr. Overbeam flapped his umbrella wings next to me. "We are dealing with very *simple* gentlemen. Besides, nothing ventured, nothing gained, young Feeb."

I ducked below the onslaught of the lethal sleeves. "Easy for you to say. You're still dry!"

He was, too. Dry as a bone nearly down to his knees. I actually considered sacrificing my second shirt for one of these outlandish Overbeam Umbrellas. At the earliest opportunity.

Robbie jiggled impatiently to my other side. "Stop wasting time, Feeb. You know the drill."

"Yes sir, Private Robson!" I smartly saluted.

Olimpio snorted. "Go. *Now*. Time passes."

We split off for the valley.

Sooner than I would've liked we met again by the cabin's front door, primed and with equipment to hand. We'd all snuck close in as silently as Olimpio. With all that pounding rain, Bog's people never noticed a thing. Armed with a shovel, I stood to one side of the door. Robbie gave me a nod, marched smartly to the door itself, and commenced beating upon it.

"Who's there?"

Robbie didn't answer, but Olimpio, crouched under the nearest shutter, let out a weird, high-pitched wail from his station. Robbie began kicking at the door.

"What in thunder is it this time—" The door swung open, and one of Bog's men stomped out, rifle to the fore. I was secreted directly to one side, and my job was easy. I clonked him smartly on the bean with the business end of the shovel. With perfect timing, Robbie caught him as he fell and hauled him around the corner to where Mr. Overbeam lay in wait, rawhide rope to hand. Olimpio wailed again.

"What's going on out there, Frank?"

Robbie imitated Frank's voice from where he was still dealing with the man himself. "You won't believe it, Bog. Come see!"

There was a grumble from within. "Told you I was comfortable. After that smoke business yesterday, I just want to rest. Have a look, Pratt."

"Sure thing, Bog."

Pratt stepped out, another rifle to the fore. I wielded the shovel a second time. Olimpio dragged this one out of sight, wailing for all he was worth. Two down. Four to go.

"Pratt! Said I didn't feel like moving. What's doing out there?"

"Never seen such a big one!" Robbie was at it again, his voice a little higher this time.

"Git out there, Travis, and haul whatever it is in, this time. An' it better be something to eat, 'cause the taters disappeared an' the bacon's all gone."

*Bonk.* Travis got his. I hoped I wasn't doing any permanent damage to anyone, but these men were so dumb they truly merited what they received. They hadn't set a guard. No one even glanced out a window. Bog certainly didn't deserve to keep Mr. Overbeam's cabin.

"Travis? Frank? Pratt!"

"Keep your pants on, boss. You'll need 'em."

"All right!" I could hear a bottle slam onto the table. "Set down your cards, boys, and we'll inspect this wonder ourselves."

"Aw, boss. Just when I got me an ace—"

The last three wandered out in a lump. I didn't need to use the shovel this time. Robbie and Olimpio already had the rifles from Frank and Pratt trained on the doorway. I relieved Bog himself of Papa's rifle.

"Won't be needing this anymore, Mr. Bog."

"What? What!"

At that moment, unable to control his curiosity any longer, Jonathan Overbeam abandoned his charges to dance by in his umbrella, flapping for all he was worth.

"*Aagh!*" shrieked one of the three. "Through the rain! It's the Condor of Death!"

Olimpio began an ululation worthy of a creature from beyond the grave.

"No—it's that last bottle of brandy. It was bad!"

"Not as bad as Overbeam's Revenge," intoned Mr. Overbeam as he pranced through the curtain of rain.

Robbie shoved his rifle into Bog's stomach. I ran into the cabin for more rope.

"What'll we do with them now, Olimpio?"

Six drenched villains, three of whom showed unmistakable signs of headaches, stood in a row before us outside the cabin. Hands were tied behind their backs. They were also roped together at the waist. I'd surely hate to try to undo the knots Mr. Overbeam had devised. Lovely, impressive constructions they were. His years as an able seaman had obviously taught him something.

I hadn't gotten an answer to my first question, so I tried a second. "What happens when all those knots get really wet from the rain, Mr. Overbeam?"

Mr. Overbeam waved his wings and chuckled. "Tighter and tighter they do get, young Feeb. Ah, the knots that bind!"

"Yer won't get away with this," Bog growled. "Yer can't!"

Robbie had a sudden thought and knelt by Bog's boots. After a quick inspection, he pulled out a knife. "Look what I found!"

Olimpio grunted and began checking the others. When the two were finished, there was quite an arsenal shining on the muddy ground before us. There were also six bags of gold dust, stolen from our creek.

"Hey! Yer can't take that gold!"

"Why not?" Mr. Overbeam inquired. "You took

my cabin, my entire valley. You've probably eaten most of my food and drunk *all* of my brandy!" It was the last that really incensed Mr. Overbeam, that was clear. He waved his wings again. "Remove them from hence, Olimpio. Far, far away. Where they can perform no further mischief." He turned to me. "Organize a suitable pack for Olimpio, Feeb. Provisions and blankets."

"What about our simple gentlemen?" I pointed.

"Well, I suppose they can have their bedrolls. Wouldn't want their fleas anyhow."

"Food?" I inquired again.

"Don't press me, Feeb. They've already consumed their share."

"But I don't think they have the same sort of survival skills that Olimpio taught us—"

"All right!" he snapped. "A little flour and beans."

I got the provisions together, handed Olimpio his pack, and slung a sack over Bog's shoulder. "You'd better steer clear in future, Mr. Bog. I'd hate to *truly* get on Mr. Overbeam's bad side. I suspect he could become even more ornery than you."

Bog didn't choose to answer. It was a sad and sorry group of rogues Robbie and I watched Olimpio escort from our valley.

Mr. Overbeam didn't waste any time on good-byes. He shot straight for the cabin. When Robbie and I finally squished our way inside, he was in mourning over the last bottle of brandy.

"All of it!" He tipped the empty bottle over the table. A lone drop splashed onto an ace of spades lying on its surface. "Those rapscallions consumed my entire stock!" He turned to the fireplace and came close to a shriek as he dashed for the mantel-shelf. "My Shakespeare!" He hugged the bedraggled volume to his chest. "Those, those *infidels*! They've been using the Bard as tinder!"

Robbie inspected the remainder of the room. "That's not all they did."

"Nope," I had to agree. "As bad as my worst estimates, the place is."

The chaos around us was so outstanding that Robbie voiced what I'd only been thinking.

"I almost wish we could stay in the cave."

Mr. Overbeam sadly relinquished his depleted Shakespeare to the tabletop and tossed the empty brandy bottle onto the pile of debris on the floor. "El Dorado Two did have a certain ambience."

"Genuine art, as well," I added. Then I squared my shoulders. "As we're already wet as we can get, I guess we'd better start lugging out all those empty sardine and peach tins."

# SEVEN

*O*limpio returned from his errand three days later, swathed in his sleeping blankets. He shrugged them off near the fireplace where they lay, steaming soggily.

"Cold comes early. Snow soon."

"What happened with Bog, Olimpio?"

"Bog and men fine, Feeb. Leave with food and one knife. Far away to north. Take all winter before find Sutter's Fort."

"What about El Dorado?" Robbie asked. "How long before they find *us* again?"

Olimpio shrugged. "Them not smart. But we keep watch. In case."

I could tell Mr. Overbeam was delighted to have his companion back. All the while he'd been listening he was scooping soup from the bubbling caldron over the fire.

"Here, my friend. It's good food and not fine words that you'll be needing now. I present you with Feeb's best pea soup, nectar of the gods themselves!"

Olimpio dug in.

Well, the four of us sat around and stared at each other for a few days. Then the snow came and we stared at that for a few more days. We'd retrieved our belongings from the cave, and I organized the little cabin till there wasn't a solitary thing left to organize. Even Mama would have started turning mad with all this confined domesticity.

It came to a head one night as I was tossing in my bedroll. Robbie began tossing next to me. We both sat up. Robbie peered through the dim light of the banked fire to make certain that Olimpio and Mr. Overbeam were truly asleep. Various snorts and snores soon attested to that fact. Tentatively, Robbie stretched out a hand. My own wandered into his. We eased flat back onto the floor, still hanging on. It felt good after all this time.

"What do you suppose the date is, Phoebe?" His voice was husky and low. "Toward the end of November, maybe?"

"Something like that. Possibly even December already. I forgot to keep track like my friend Miss Prendergast used to on the Oregon Trail."

"That leaves maybe four months before we can get back to mining."

I stared straight up at the rafters above. The tiniest flicker of light glanced from them. "If we're lucky, and the spring isn't as wet as this autumn was."

"Another week of snow and we'll never get out of this valley until the thaw."

"That thought has occurred to me, Robbie."

He squeezed my fingers absently. "Gold's not all it's cracked up to be, Phoebe."

"I noticed that, too." I squeezed back, not so absently. "You ever figure that maybe we've got enough to book passage home? If we took our share from Bog?"

"Yup. In time for the spring planting, like we promised our folks."

"It wouldn't be dishonorable to leave now, would it, Robbie? Now that Mr. Overbeam's all set for the winter, with Olimpio to look after him?"

"I can't see how, Phoebe. We stay around here a few more months, we'll be sticking knives in each other, same as Bog's men would've."

"Even Mr. Overbeam's latest project, trying to teach us *Macbeth* by heart, wouldn't save us from—"

I broke off as Robbie's fingers changed their pressure, began to trace my blood-sister scar.

"Out, damned spot, out!" I caught myself declaiming in a theatrical whisper. It wasn't that I wanted that scar out, ever. It was thinking about Lady Macbeth slowly going crazy. It made me shiver involuntarily. Why had Mr. Overbeam chosen a tragedy for us to act out? Probably because it was the only play still intact in his book. The shiver worked its way down my arm to my fingers. Robbie pulled his hand away to prop it under his head.

"Dangerous. That's what this situation could turn into."

"Subversive," I agreed.

"We'll talk it out in the morning." He leaned over and planted a kiss on my cheek. "Good night, Phoebe."

It hadn't been that much of a kiss, but the spot he'd touched with his lips kept me awake most of the night with its tingling.

I set a stack of pancakes on the table, then added the jug of molasses. "Mr. Overbeam?" I started.

"Feeb and I—" Robbie added.

"—Have been doing some thinking," I finished.

"An excellent enterprise." Mr. Overbeam deftly flipped three huge cakes onto his plate and made a grab for the molasses. It was a wonder how he stayed so skinny, the way the man ate. "Highly to be recommended."

"About the winter—" I tried again.

"—And being snowed in here—"

Olimpio helped himself to his own stack. "Robbie and Feeb have ants," he observed. "Cannot winter like Indian."

"Thank you, Olimpio. That's exactly what we were trying to say."

Mr. Overbeam poured molasses atop his pancakes until they were swimming. Then he added more. Finally he set down the jug. "Do I detect mutiny in the ranks?"

"Far from it, sir," Robbie protested. "We've enjoyed every moment of our time with you. It's been . . ."

"Educational," I threw in. "It's been positively educational!" I finally got my hands on the syrup and spread a little around my own breakfast. "We're just not convinced that being snowed in for four months is the best use of our time."

"Ah, so it's civilization, the bright lights of San Francisco that call to you?"

"More like the fields of Oregon Territory and home, Mr. Overbeam," Robbie clarified.

"You'd give up your shares in our Mother Lode?"

"What's gold done for us so far?" I asked. "Only gotten us attacked and robbed and—"

"And taught you a few survival skills, my dear Feeb. Never forget that!"

"No, Mr. Overbeam." My pancakes were usually pretty fair, but right now they tasted like sawdust in my mouth. Mr. Overbeam finally sighed and turned to Olimpio.

"Would you be opposed to leading our associates back to Sutter's Fort, my friend?"

"Miss Feeb's food," Olimpio allowed. "Overbeam bad cook." He slid the last cakes onto his plate. "Leave soon. More snow coming."

Bundled in our blankets against the cold, Robbie and I stood just inside the cabin door. Mr. Overbeam fussed over us.

"Did you pack enough food? . . . How about your gold pans? Never can tell when a strike might sneak up on you. . . . Will Bog's gold dust be enough to get you safely home? . . . Are you certain your match safes are dry?"

We answered yes to everything, then still stood waiting, unwilling at the last moment to leave.

Mr. Overbeam rubbed at his nose, pulled his ears a little more askew. The tassel of his nightcap jerked convulsively. "You're welcome back in the spring, should your minds be changed. Remember that, my friends. Two quarters of El Dorado are still legally yours!"

"Thank you, Mr. Overbeam. And do consider Oregon City for your little house and library. We've even got a Literary Society—"

Olimpio thrust his head through the doorway. "Come. Now. Weather changes."

Mr. Overbeam gave me a hug, then reached for Robbie's hand. "Do take care of your young la—er, *cousin*, my dear giant. More precious than all the Mother Lodes in the world, our Feeb is."

Robbie blanched, then managed to answer, "I'll try, sir. My very best."

While I was still working out how Mr. Overbeam had seen through my disguise, Robbie hauled at me, and we were off again.

It snowed all the way down the Sierras to the foothills. By the time we neared Sutter's Mill it was slacking off. By Sutter's Fort it was raining. We made our farewells to Olimpio and left him purchasing lime juice, peaches, and brandy for Mr. Overbeam. We hardly took in the new town of Sacramento that'd sprung up outside the fort in our absence. Hardly took in any of the changes wrought, we were that anxious to board a waiting launch for the trip back to San Francisco.

The launch wasn't full for the return journey, and we managed to avail ourselves of a small corner of the boat's main and only cabin saloon, and even to pay for the poor fare that was slopped out three times a day. By the time we reached San Francisco Bay, the fog hovering over the Golden Gate actually looked welcoming. We staggered ashore.

Robbie surveyed the town. "Well, here we are again, Feeb. But it seems different."

"I'll say."

San Francisco had been nearly a ghost town when we'd left it. Now it was surrounded by a second town of tents perched haphazardly over the surrounding hills. Hammers rang out everywhere as new buildings rose. The streets bustled with miners of every color of the rainbow. They must have just arrived in California, or just returned from the diggings for the winter, like us. There were even a few women walking near Central Wharf and the bay on Front Street.

"Look at that lady." I nudged at Robbie. "Doesn't she seem *exotic*?"

Robbie steered me in another direction. "I'm not absolutely certain, Feeb, but I suspect she ain't a lady."

"Oh." Things had changed. Fast. "What do we do now?"

"Find out about a ship for home."

Finding a ship for home was easier said than done. It wasn't because there was a dearth of ships, either. San Francisco harbor was filled with ships—abandoned, every last one of them. Their masts stuck up like a small forest growing over the water. And not a captain or sailor to be found. The two of us walked for hours questioning people. The answers were always the same.

"Oregon? Who'd want to go back to Oregon? Half the Territory's here already!"

"Only ships moving are bound south, to pick up them eastern argonauts waitin' by Panama City. Waitin' to join in on the rush."

"But—" I protested, "nobody can dig for another four months! It's winter!"

"Gonna have to winter in San Francisco like everybody else, sonny."

By the end of the day, Robbie and I were almost ready to accept the truth. Ready, but not yet resigned.

"We can start in searching again for a way home first thing tomorrow, Robbie. Right now, my legs are about to fall off. I'm not used to walking in a city. Not one with all these hills." I shook a booted foot disconsolately. It weighed about thirty extra pounds from all the muck caked to it. "And not one with unpaved streets filled with mud holes." I twisted around for another inspection of the hastily built one- and two-story structures surrounding us. "And not a single tree, Robbie. Not even any shrubs left on the hills. I didn't notice that first time through, but coming straight from the mountains like we just did—"

"Probably cut it all down for firewood." Robbie leaned wearily against the nearest unpainted clapboard shack. "We'll have to find a place to stay, Feeb. All this fog feels unhealthy. Not clean like the snows up in El Dorado."

"We'll have to pay, too," I lamented. "And it won't come cheap."

Dear is what it was, and not in Mr. Overbeam's sense of the word, either. We finally located one tiny, empty chamber in a two-story lodging house halfway up Telegraph Hill.

"How much?" I asked, in fear and trembling.

"Fifty dollars a month. In advance."

"What if we don't want to stay a month?"

"It's still fifty dollars. One night or the whole length." The proprietor turned to spit out his front door into the muddy street. "Don't make no nevermind to me. The room's only vacant on account of its last occupant just expired of scurvy from the hills. Be a dozen others willing to take it this night."

"Is the—uh—*body* gone?"

Robbie poked me into silence. Three scruffy miners were starting up the front steps behind us. "We'll take it."

Fifty dollars' worth of our gold dust having been weighed out in the front room, we climbed the steps to our new abode. I breathed a sigh of relief. The body was gone. Unfortunately, everything else was, too. The room hadn't a stick of furniture in it, not even a mattress. There wasn't any fireplace, either.

Robbie dropped his pack. It thudded hollowly on the bare planks of the floor. The gold bag still in one hand looked even hollower. "Half our money's gone, Feeb. I don't believe there's enough left for passage home. And I don't think I'd be willing to try stowing away again." His shoulder blades jerked in sudden memory. "We'll have to get jobs and save up."

"We still have to eat, too."

Robbie kneeled to unpack the last of our emergency provisions from Mr. Overbeam. "Here. Have some smoked elk to chew on. It's kept Olimpio alive for years."

The two of us sat there gnawing at the last of our elk. Out of the frying pan and into the fire is where we'd gotten ourselves. A cold, burned-out fire. It was a discouraging moment.

Surprisingly, there were still jobs to be had in San Francisco. First thing in the morning, Robbie was taken on as a carpenter for the half-built Parker House Hotel growing out of several city lots. Twenty dollars a day were offered for his services. It was an incredible wage for Oregon, but we could have panned that much out of Blackwater Creek in half an hour. Before the rains.

I left him and wandered about the waking town, seeking my own employment. It was small wonder there were still jobs. Every second building was slapped together from canvas and a few planks— and practically all of these establishments were either whiskey saloons or gambling houses. They were already beginning to bustle for the day, too. Then again, maybe they'd never shut down all night. A barker stood before one of them, eyeing me as I paused.

"Right here, my fine young sir. Step right up! Here's a monte bank that'll stand you a rip!"

"What's monte?"

"What's monte, the lad asks? Why, only the finest

game of chance in California! Just match a face-up card with the dealer's and you've won!" He reached for my collar. "Don't be shy, stake up to win your fortune!"

"No thanks." I slipped from his grasp. "Got to have something to bet with first, don't I?"

The barker's interest in me died swiftly. He turned to the next victims walking down the street. "Pungle 'er down right here, gents! The best monte in San Francisco!"

As I continued on my way, my stomach began to grumble in protest—just like it used to when provisions were way down on the Oregon Trail. There weren't any wild creatures to be bagged in San Francisco, though. Only the two-legged variety. As if in sympathy with my stomach, my legs stopped walking right in front of another canvas tent. Greasy fumes reeked from its open flaps, and a sign tacked above the entrance read: *Ma Jones's Grub*. It also had something else scribbled right beneath: *Help Wanted*.

I glanced around quickly, to see if anyone was running up after that job. No one seemed to be. *Lord,* I offered up. *Lord, I'm hungry. And Olimpio did say I could cook. Help me out again, please?* Thus bolstered, I squared my shoulders and strode between the flaps.

Two long tables were spread with what passed for food. About a dozen men were chowing down. Toward the rear of the tent a bear of a man leaned over a steaming pot, the cigar firmly clamped between his teeth casually drifting its ashes into the fixings.

"What'll it be?" he roared.

"I'm . . . I'm searching for Ma Jones."

"You're looking at him, kid. In the flesh."

Of course. And why not? Everything else around this town was insane, wasn't it? I tried out a brave smile and propelled myself a few steps closer. "I understand you could use some help, sir."

He stared me up and down, once. This time the cigar ashes drifted over his beard onto his gut. "If you're offering, it's ten dollars the day and all the food you can eat."

I gulped at the latter, unsure whether that was good news or bad. It didn't matter. "Where do I start?"

Ma Jones nodded at the closest table. "Clear off them leavings and wash up the dishes out back."

"Yes, sir." My first paying job had officially begun.

# EIGHT

*O*ne week into our San Francisco sojourn, Robbie and I sat propped against a bare wall in our room. It was late at night. Working hours didn't seem to have any fixed limit in this town. We were counting up the gold dust and coins we'd accumulated in seven days.

"It's not too bad, Phoebe," Robbie assessed. "With you feeding me and yourself both from Ma Jones, we haven't had food expenses."

"Nor any other. We could use some extra blankets, though. It's draftier than my loft back home up here. And danker." I hugged my blanket more tightly around me. "We could both use warm coats, too. I worry about you outside all day."

"Don't, Feb. I'm usually in a sweat anyhow." He jiggled the loose coins. "Two hundred and ten dollars we've made already."

"I know. I don't like you carrying it around in your money pouch, either. The men around here are on to that trick."

"You have a better idea of what to do with it?"

I hesitated. Maybe I had. Not that Robbie would be expecting any sort of an answer. I grabbed his hand for strength—and maybe to lessen the lunacy of the proposal—before spilling my idea. "I might. A way to invest it, so to speak."

Robbie gave my fingers an encouraging squeeze. Emboldened, I continued.

"I've been thinking about all this, Robbie, letting the idea take shape and build for seven long days. . . ."

Seven long days while I scurried around under Ma Jones's thumb. Turned out his real name was Hank, but everyone called him "Ma" now, and he seemed to take a certain pride in the appellation. Once he'd figured out that I was dependable, and bright to boot, he'd started sending me off after supplies. In one short week I'd pretty much figured out the system working between the suppliers and shop owners and the rest of us in San Francisco—the dupers versus the dupes, so to speak. Those of us in the unfortunate majority were just as much victims as if we'd spent all our waking hours in monte parlors.

I turned through the dark to try to catch Robbie's eyes. "Already I've had my fill of Ma Jones. I believe you've had enough of the carpentry business, too. If we're going to be stuck here for the duration—" I took a deep breath, then finally let it out. "It's time to stop being sheep and join up with the goats, Robbie. Fact of the matter is, I think we should start a restaurant." There. It was out. I'd done it.

Robbie dropped my hand and stared back at me, just trying to grasp the idea. "A *restaurant*? You out of your mind, Feeb?"

"Hardly. We'll call it Mother Phoebe's Restaurant." I spread my arms in the darkness to encompass the idea. "'Home Cooking Guaranteed.' Listen, Robbie. Jones gets three dollars straight up for breakfast. Four for dinner and supper. That's eleven dollars a day from hungry men, every day of the week. And in case you hadn't noticed, there's a lot of them out there. I figure on giving them a break. Every man who signs up for an entire week can have his meals for sixty dollars flat. Maybe even less, once we're organized. You can help me get set up, and advertise, and look after the supplies. . . ." I petered out.

"You're really serious about this, ain't you?"

"Dead serious."

Robbie thought hard. He was long on things like patience and virtue and dependability, but sometimes short on imagination. Still, after the adventures we'd already shared, I'd back him with my money anytime.

"We'd need a stake, Feeb. For buying the tent, and renting a lot to set it on, and then there's a stove—"

"They've got loan men in San Francisco, Robbie."

"You'd trust them, after hearing Mr. Overbeam and Shakespeare on the subject?"

"Trusting them wasn't what I had in mind. As long as we can keep up with our pound of flesh—"

"You're really set to do this." His mind was struggling over the leap from the impossible to the possible. The leap of faith.

"I am, indeed, Robbie. Until one of those lumber ships comes through from Oregon."

He sat there cracking his knuckles, one by one. It was a recent habit. I wasn't sure how much I really hated it yet.

"When do you want to get started?"

"First thing tomorrow morning, of course!"

San Francisco was a booming town, a town built on hopes and dreams and fresh ideas. Our idea wasn't as fresh as all that, but even the moneylenders could see its merits. Our particular moneylender was one Sam Brannan, who'd forsaken Mormonism for the wiles of the world. He was probably the richest man in the city—so far—at least according to Ma Jones, who was trying mightily to emulate him. Ma was never going to make it. He just wasn't in the same league.

Brannan was all smoothness to Ma Jones's roughness: sleek black hair, smoothly shaved cheeks, tight belly encased in an embroidered vest. He listened to our pitch with hardly any impatience for such a busy man. When we'd finished, he leaned back in the polished chair of his well-appointed office and thought for a split second. Then he reached into a drawer of the desk before him. He pulled out a sheet of paper and scribbled on it.

"There." He presented the sheet to us. "Our contract. I won't loan you the money. I'll put it up outright—in return for a fifty percent share."

"Fifty percent!" I spluttered. "That's highway robbery! We'll be doing all the labor! Getting all the clients! Working ourselves to the bone!"

Brannan drummed his fingers on the desk between us. "I presently own all of the outstanding vacant lots in San Francisco. At my discretion I may sell, rent, or utilize these lots—or not. At my discretion. Also—" His drumming stopped as he stared us down across the space. "I get thirty men a day lining up for a piece of my investment money. All of them with big ideas."

Well, we knew for a fact that was true. Hadn't we waited in line half the day for our own turn with Brannan?

"Forty percent," Robbie spoke up. "It ain't fair, but it's fairer."

Brannan smiled, teeth bright and just a little sharp. "Forty-five."

I turned to Robbie. He cracked a knuckle.

"All right, Mr. Brannan," I allowed. "I guess you've got us up a creek."

Brannan stuck his pen in the inkwell, scratched out the 50 percent on the contract, and changed it to 45 percent. "Let's have your John Hancocks right here."

Robbie signed first, his name in full: Robert Sturdevant Robson. I signed underneath: F. B. Brown. I suppose that wasn't exactly legal, but what was in this town? If I were wearing skirts, I wouldn't be signing at all. Women hadn't won the right to sign anything yet. Sam Brannan handed us each a cigar to close the deal, and we decamped.

Funny thing about Sam Brannan's name. It opened doors everywhere. In three days I was cooking my first meal inside the tent of Mother

Phoebe's. Robbie had plastered signs all over town about our grand new enterprise, and there were already twenty men in line for my breakfast pancakes, paying by the meal instead of the week, checking out the goods before they committed themselves. Five of them were satisfied enough to sign on after they'd stuffed themselves to the gills and beyond. Dinner was more hectic, and supper worse still. By then the word had gotten around that Mother Phoebe could cook, and I had to scrape the bottom of the pots to keep bowls filled with Mr. Overbeam's favorite—pea soup.

Robbie and I sank onto benches across a table from each other at the end of that first day. The tent flaps were closed and a single lantern lit the cavernous space. I pulled up the edge of my food-splattered apron to mop at my face. "I think we did it."

Robbie started to crack a knuckle, then stopped. Instead, he reached his hand across for mine. "*You* did it, Phoebe. I knew you had it in you, but cooking for four at El Dorado is a whole sight different from cooking for a hundred or so in San Francisco."

"Wouldn't my mama be proud of me. Wouldn't Amelia be shocked! As for Papa—"

"Your papa should have figured out by this time that you can accomplish anything you set your mind to."

I shook myself out of self-congratulations. "Which reminds me. I've got a menu to work out for tomorrow. You notice the men asking for oysters today, Robbie? You'll have to head down to the water before daybreak tomorrow and buy us a slew. Ma Jones said as how the entire bay is starting to be raked up." I shook my head. "Not that I can stomach them raw, the way most of these men love them, but oyster stew would take care of tomorrow night's soup."

"How we doing on steaks, Feeb?" Robbie had already dropped my hand to get back to business. He pulled out the little notebook he'd purchased to keep track of things and began to scribble in it. I'd been right about him again. Once he figured out what he was responsible for, nothing interfered with business.

"Better order in six dozen for tomorrow. And about nine dozen eggs, and more butter, and—" The list went on. I finally halted, my whole body leaning into my elbows on the roughly cobbled table. It *was* rough. "Tablecloths. Tablecloths would add a little class to this place."

"Where in thunder are we supposed to find tablecloths, Feeb?"

"Check the dry goods at Sam Brannan's store. Worse comes to worst, we can use linen sheets."

"That'll be extra expenses for laundry work. You saw the way these men eat, Feeb. Like hogs at the trough."

"We give them tablecloths, maybe their standards will improve a little. Speaking of which . . ." For the first time in months I noticed Robbie's frayed sleeves. "Take the time to stop in that haberdashery tomorrow, Robbie. Get yourself fixed up with some duds like Sam Brannan wears." I studied him more closely. "You might consider a haircut, too. You're the side of the business people see, so we've got to put on a prosperous front."

"What about you, Feeb?"

I glanced down at Papa's badly aging leftovers. No question that trousers were comfortable and easy to get around in. Still, there was that in me beginning to cry out for the softness of petticoats and skirts. For the luxury of feeling my hair long and full again. For the end of this male charade. Thus far, Mr. Overbeam was the only one who'd caught on, but then he was entirely perspicacious, and entirely the gentleman. . . . My head shook of

its own volition. Such a transformation would mark
the end of my little business enterprise. San Francisco wasn't yet ready for legitimate females.

"I guess these will do for a little while yet. At
least until I find me some hired help and can sneak
out for a few minutes."

"Hired help," Robbie muttered and proceeded
to scratch in his notebook. "I'll look into that
tomorrow, too."

I tried stretching, but I was that exhausted it
hurt. "Let's go home, Robbie, before I make a bed
of this tabletop."

The oysters arrived first the next morning.
Shortly on their heels came my hired help. Robbie
had been busy. Customers hadn't even started
coming in for breakfast yet, so I was startled when
I heard a voice inquiring after "Mother Phoebe." I
jumped away from my vast new cast-iron stove.

"I guess that's me. At least, I'm Feeb."

A famished-looking old man with less height
than I stood before me, scuffed hat nervously in
hand. Well, maybe he wasn't all that old, but the
wild tufts of his curly hair had already gone gray.
My eyes dropped down to his feet. A mangy, fur-
matted mutt sat there, tail slowly a-wag, two short
little ears almost askew as Mr. Overbeam's. It was

those ears that did it. "What can I do for you two?"

"Mr. Robson sent us." The dog barked, once, in agreement. "Said you was looking for good help."

Whatever had possessed Robbie? I glanced at that dog again. "I guess I am looking. For *good* help. Ten dollars the day, and all the food you and your friend can eat."

A glorious smile lit up both face and muzzle. I swear.

"I'm Amos, and my associate here is known as Esau, for he is hairy."

"Does Esau like eggs?"

"We both love 'em. Raw, hard-boiled, scrambled, or any other fashion."

"Well, let's start with breakfast, then."

Once fed, Esau curled up under the warmth of my huge stove. Amos turned into a marvel.

"What if I start with the oysters, Mr. Feeb?"

"Feeb will do, Amos."

"What if I start with the oysters, Feeb? Not everybody knows the trick of cracking 'em open and setting them out handsome on a bed of ice like in a fine New York restaurant."

"Where will we get the ice?" I stopped. "You've been to New York?"

"Worked in some of them fine restaurants. Until Esau and me got the urge to wander and took on cooking for one of them round-the-Horn schooners. When we made Valparaíso in Chile we got wind of the gold rush. Them Chileños scurried aboard like rats for passage north. Our ship, she's laying out in the bay this minute, abandoned like the rest. Now me and Esau just have to make it through the winter."

His first words shook me enough that I hardly followed the rest. The man knew oysters. The man was a *cook*. Robbie was a wonder. "You have any favorite recipes, Amos?"

He'd slipped out a knife and was already working on the first bushel of oysters as we talked. "I can concoct a mean lobscouse and dandy funk that'll take your breath away. But my true specialités lie with them Frenchie sauces that were big in New York when we took off."

My hands were still idle, and I was working hard to keep my mouth from gaping like a prime idiot. "What kind of sauces might those be, Amos?"

"Oh, Madeira, à la Chambord, hollandaise; I can do a pretty fair galantine, too. I was never more than a sous-chef, mind you, but I always kept my eyes open, and I've a certain knack."

I had no idea what a galantine might be. Nor a sous-chef, either. I was almost afraid to ask. At that moment, however, the tent flaps parted.

"Is this here Mother Phoebe's? Cain't read a word, but if it is, I've come for breakfast, and brought my partners!"

Four burly men plunked themselves down to table. I found a smile for them. "It certainly is, gentlemen. Eggs sunnyside up or easy over?"

Another day had begun.

Those oysters turned out to be a big hit. They'd been swallowed raw, fried, and in a stew. The relish with which they'd disappeared still amazed me, as did the joking that went along with their consumption. My customers were a wild and rowdy bunch to be sure, and more than once I found myself blessing Papa's trousers and shirts that so effectively disguised me.

Not that all my customers were jolly and good-natured. There were always a few malcontents in any crowd. My prime lemon for the day—a tall, cadaverous soul with the scowl of permanent heartburn—turned up at supper, tossed down his coins, and hunched off to a table to sink his nose into my oyster stew. I stood at the counter that divided the kitchen area from the dining area, ladling stew into the next bowl. My head jerked up when I heard an outraged howl.

"You clod! What in tarnation you doin' emptyin'

your stew atop my trousers!" The gentleman next to Mr. Lemon glared indignantly at the perpetrator.

"'Cause that's where it belongs!" growled Mr. Lemon. "No slop with only four ersters in it ought to be called erster stew!"

"Well, why you takin' it up with me?" The second man was already on his feet, trying to dance off the scalding soup. "It's Mother Phoebe over there you should be complainin' to!"

"I took it up with you 'cause you were idiot enough to eat it!"

"Call me an idiot, will you?" A knife flashed ominously out of nowhere.

But I was already under the counter and into the dining area, Papa's rifle to hand. The knife disappeared as I cocked and pointed the gun at the appropriate body, totally ignoring the stares of my other diners. None of them needed to know that the weapon was unloaded.

"He's right, Mr. Lemon. You have a problem, you bring it directly to me. And now that you've got my undivided attention, talk!"

He shambled to his feet, glaring. "Back where I come from, there's so many ersters in a stew, you got to cut through 'em to find the soup. Back where I come from, a man don't get robbed every minute by saloons and gambling parlors, and over-priced lodging houses. Most of all, he don't get robbed by no so-called restaurant!"

I kept my arms steady on the rifle, even though they were beginning to ache a little. It had been a fair amount of time since I'd actually needed to aim it at anything, after all. It was only behind the counter to begin with as a "deterrent," as Robbie had put it. I allowed my trigger finger to twitch a little. "Then maybe you should've stayed back where you came from. You have any idea what the going rate is for oysters in San Francisco, Mr. Lemon?"

"No!" he spat out. "And where'd that 'Lemon' business come from? My name's always been Hicks, and always will be!"

"The Lemon comes from your disposition, Mr. Hicks." I nodded briefly around. "Doesn't that seem appropriate, gentlemen?"

My other customers, who were beginning to enjoy the unexpected free entertainment with their meal, yelled out vociferous agreement.

"Right you are, Feeb!"

"Let him have it! Pucker 'im right up!"

"This here stew's better than my old gray-haired ma's!"

"Amen!"

The rifle was feeling heavy again, and I had other customers still waiting. Best to finish this business. "For your information, Mr. *Lemon* Hicks, oysters go for two bits apiece. That means you tossed an entire dollar's worth on your neighbor's trousers. Now if you add in two dollars for the steak you would have been eating next, and another dollar for the trimmings, that would have given you a four-dollar meal. If you can find oysters cheaper than that in San Francisco, you bring them to me, and I'll fix up a stew to your specifications."

I lowered the barrel slightly. "In the meantime I'll have to ask you to leave my place of business. Mother Phoebe's caters meals, not rowdyism."

Hicks slunk off to myriad lemon-tinged catcalls. I feared the man would be living with his new name for some time. For the present, though, I personally refilled and served another bowl of stew to his unfortunate victim—this bowl swimming with oysters. It was gulped with relish, and before leaving, Mr. Lemon Hicks's victim signed up for my full weekly service. I'm not certain whether it was for the food, or the sport, but most of the other men did, too.

After supper was finished at last and Amos and I had cleaned up, I sat for the first time all day to think. Amos and Esau were curled together in a corner of the tent, asleep. Apparently they'd found a home.

I smoothed the folds of a tablecloth I'd only just spread for the first time. Supplies had been arriving all day, the linen sheets last and too late for the final meal. What had not arrived all day was Robbie. Certainly there'd been constant signs of his diligence, but I was hungry for sight of the young man himself. He might have been useful during that oyster episode, too. Just in case the affair had escalated. Where in the world could he be?

I absently traced designs into the fabric of the linen with my fingertip. Designs like the map of scars on Robbie's back. No doubt I could keep this little business going on my own, now that it was up and running. All it seemed to take was nonstop endurance and a firm hand with the customers. But it was Robbie who was busy smoothing the way for me. What in the world would I do without Robbie? Fifteen hours I hadn't seen him, and already I missed him. What was happening to me?

A gust of dank air blew across my face and I raised my head. Someone was standing there halfway through parted tent flaps. Someone I didn't recognize.

"We're closed till tomorrow. Sorry."

"Phoebe? It's me!"

I stared again. An incredibly handsome young man was walking toward me—tall, blond, resplendent in ruffled shirt and softly knotted tie. A veritable *dandy*. "Robbie?"

He fussed with the lapels of his plum-colored frock coat. "Well, you ordered me to get spruced up, Feeb! I'm sorry it took so long, but what with the new clothes, and the bath and shave and haircut . . ."

"Oh, Robbie!"

Maybe it had to do with being exhausted. Maybe it had to do with the leftover strain from the oyster mutiny. Anyhow, then and there I broke the promise I'd made to him so long ago back in Oregon. The promise about giving no open signs of affection. I threw myself into his arms.

# NINE

*W*hen an Oregon ship laden with planks for lumber-hungry San Francisco finally sailed into the bay several weeks later, Robbie and I did not rush to board it for home. How could we? We were businessmen with responsibilities.

Mother Phoebe's had expanded. We were feeding upwards of two hundred men, three times a day. At a commitment of sixty dollars the week for each of them, that put a lot of money in our hands—even after Sam Brannan took his cut and we'd paid out our other expenses.

"More than twelve thousand dollars, Robbie!" We were staring at the week's grosses after another long day. "It hardly seems real. I never imagined there was this much money in the world! Not even when Mr. Overbeam found his gold vein. If I hadn't worked so hard, it would feel like stealing."

Robbie wasn't all that impressed. He swept it into the leather satchel he'd taken to carrying for making disbursements to our creditors. "What about that Oregon ship, Feeb?"

"The Oregon ship?" I pulled a thick envelope from an inside pocket of my new frock coat. Peacock blue it was, and only suitable for wearing when I wasn't cooking. I rather enjoyed the feel of the soft wool. I tapped the envelope against a leg neatly sheathed in fawn cord, tapered—as was the current fashion—over the ankles of my handmade polished boots. The rest of my new wardrobe wasn't anywhere near as elegant as Robbie's, but it had improved commensurate to my status. At least with a good tailor I needn't roll up my trouser legs any longer. I'd had the ragged edges of my hair trimmed, too. "It's sailing back tomorrow, isn't it? The ship. To Fort Vancouver. I've written up a long letter for Mama and Papa, so they can stop worrying for a while."

Robbie stared at his fingers. I knew he was thinking about cracking a knuckle. He'd been too busy to perform that little gesture of worry lately. "We do have employees to take into account now. And it's nowhere near planting season yet. I suppose I'd better scribble something for my ma and pa, too."

"That would be considerate, Robbie."

He sat there, toying with the fob of the gold watch I'd gotten him for Christmas while he studied that envelope now lying between us. He certainly

didn't look like any Oregon Territory man I'd ever
seen. Not anymore. That watch and fob had just
about completed his transformation into a brand-
new kind of male—not a farmer or a miner, but a
*San Francisco* man. I was still a little unsure of what
the two of us had wrought.

"Robbie?"

"Yes?"

"Are we taking all that money home with us
tonight?"

"It should be safe enough. It's always been before. Only real problems we've ever had have been
right here during mealtimes. And you solved most
of them, between those civilizing tablecloths—and
word getting around about your steady aim." He
pulled at the fob some more until the watch itself
was dangling from the end of it and swaying back
and forth, back and forth.

"What's the matter, Robbie?"

His eyes seemed unable to rise beyond the level
of the watch's arc. "I've done something, Feeb. I
know we always talked everything out between us,
before. . . ."

My heart began thumping uncomfortably. Even
with Amos promoted to sous-chef, even with ten
waiters and dishwashers scurrying around at my
bidding, I still didn't have the time to leave the

restaurant much. Robbie continued to take care of all the details that kept us running smoothly, even as quantities increased. Was he losing interest in it all? Did he really want to return to Oregon that badly? Or worse still, had he taken a fancy to one of those *ladies* that promenaded so brazenly around the city? He had plenty of money in his pockets to burn . . . the possibilities were endless. I bit the bullet.

"What, Robbie? What have you done?"

He dropped the watch to muss his perfectly barbered hair. "Well, you've been too tired for us to talk properly lately, like we always used to."

"And?" I prompted.

"And I wasn't sure just exactly how badly you still wanted to go back to the homestead in Oregon. . . . I mean, it's not as if there's anything different to do there, Feeb. Just more plowing . . . and things are sort of interesting here—"

"*What*, Robbie? For heaven's sake, spit it out!"

He gave me a sheepish grin. "Only took a page from your own book, Feeb. Made us a little investment."

"With *our* money? Without my say-so?"

"Well, it seemed like a once in a lifetime opportunity, so to speak. And if I hadn't done it, there were others standing in line." He stood up and hefted the satchel. "Come on, Feeb. I'm just putting my foot in it. Let me show you."

Robbie walked me through the nighttime streets of San Francisco, along Battery, across Broadway. Past the saloons and gambling parlors going full guns. Miners staggered through the muddy streets around us, quiet and bellicose both. I wanted to ask Robbie more as we weaved through them. I couldn't imagine in my wildest dreams what he'd gone and done with our profits.

In the end I just followed him silently along Lombard Street up Telegraph Hill. Up the steep track past our lodging place, higher still. Almost to the little semaphore station at the very top that'd given the hill its name. He finally stopped. I squinted through the blackness until a mass of clouds lifted from the face of the moon. Then I saw it. It was a three-story clapboard house built on two lots into the side of the hill. It sparkled in the moonlight with a brand-new coat of paint. Robbie finally cleared his throat.

"There you are, Feeb."

"What is it?"

"San Francisco's newest and finest lodging house. *Ours*."

"Ours?" I squeaked.

"Yup." He made for the steps. "Come along. I'll give you the tour."

We climbed the steps and across a veranda to enter a hallway lit with graceful brass oil lamps bracketed to the walls. Robbie poked his head into a room opening off one side of it. It was some kind of a fancy salon, heavy with velvet drapes. "Mrs. Meeks?" he inquired.

A matronly woman eased herself from a plush couch placed near a blazing fire. Formidable chest in advance, she sailed the distance between us, hand outstretched. "Ah, Mr. Robson. You've come at last with your partner." She fondled Robbie's hand before nearly wringing the life from mine. "And you! I've been so anxious to meet you. The entire town's abuzz with your new restaurant! Such a clever name, pulling at the heartstrings as it does! Such an efficient operation! And the womanly touch—tablecloths and even flowers! Truly inspired!" She finally relinquished my mangled fingers to lift a curious pair of glasses to her eyes— a lorgnette, as I later discovered—and study me closer. "And all accomplished by one so youthful."

"Feeb—" Robbie rushed in before I could be embarrassed further. "Mrs. Meeks is a widow from before the gold days. She's kindly offered to oversee our little establishment for us."

Mrs. Meeks was still inspecting me through those magnifying lenses. "For twenty percent, of course."

"Naturally." I swallowed hard. This was San Francisco, after all. Profits first and foremost. "My pleasure, ma'am."

Robbie propelled me in the direction of the hallway. "Let me show you the rest, the best part." He stopped. "Did everything arrive, Mrs. Meeks?"

"Oh, yes, dearie." I turned to catch her fumbling in the folds between her bosoms to produce a key. "I arranged it just as you directed."

Robbie snatched at the key. "Thank you."

What else could Robbie have up his sleeve? I followed him to the top floor, wondering. He paused before a closed door and flourished the key.

"I hope you like it, Feeb. I picked the top because of the view. You can see clear across the bay on a nice day." He swept open the door.

A little sitting room, perfectly appointed with softly upholstered furniture and a warming fire, met my eyes.

"What is all this, Robbie?"

"Home. I thought it was time to improve our lodgings." He smiled suddenly, then grabbed my hand, like in the old days. "Just wait till you see our bedrooms!"

There were two of them, each with a massive bedstead. I wandered between the two, then bounced on the mattress in my room. "It's not cornhusks, or fir boughs, or anything else. It's a real mattress! It's been *years* since I've slept on a real mattress. Since Massachusetts. I'd forgotten they existed!"

Robbie stood in the doorway watching me bounce. "Is it all right then, Feeb? What I did?"

I bounced another time. "A real wardrobe for my clothes—"

"Rosewood, Feeb, with genuine brass handles. The dresser and chest, too. Spirited off a China clipper."

"Is the fireplace from China, too?" I teased. "And the fire?"

"You don't like them? I thought sure—"

The sudden distress on his broad face brought me back to earth. "I love them, Robbie. It's just all so sudden. And more *permanent* than anything we've done before. . . . A scary sort of permanent . . . although I suppose those Oregon ships will be coming regular from now on. Won't they? At the price they're getting for lumber—"

"They'd be fools not to come," he said.

"And we can send letters home with each ship."

"Until we've had enough, or the rush is over."

I leaned back against the headboard and threw my booted feet, mud and all, right atop the fancy counterpane. "Fair enough. Until we've had enough, or the rush is over."

Robbie lounged against the doorjamb, beaming. "I know it's way past the proper date, but it finally feels right to me. Happy New Year, Phoebe. Happy 1849."

"Just let me in on the next surprise, Robbie."

He opened his mouth, but whatever he was going to reply never came out. Instead, there was a sudden commotion. A sort of knocking and scratching both. My feet flew off the bedcovers almost guiltily.

"What's that?"

"It sounded like someone at our door."

"Who would know—"

But Robbie was already loping toward the door. I followed as he pulled it open. A ball of fur flew into my arms.

"Esau!"

"And Amos. Mr. Robson, Feeb." The curly gray head tilted back so he could smile up at us. "A housewarming being a special occasion, I took the liberty—"

"Whatever is that you're carrying, Amos?"

He thrust a large platter at me, causing the

mutt to make a flying leap from my embrace.

"One of my galantines, Feeb. Mrs. Meeks kindly allowed me to construct it in her kitchen, seeing as how Mr. Robson got Esau and me a room here. In the midst of the highest society we ever mingled with. Got a Mr. Goodman to one side what's come to set up a new bank, and a genuine high-toned lawyer to the other. Coziest little room you ever seen, too. Not that we minded the restaurant's floor, Esau and me, but the new place is much warmer. And Esau is that fond of a good mattress."

Amos bustled over to the sitting room fire, rubbed his hands before it, then turned expectantly. "A new home ought to be celebrated among friends, oughtn't it?"

I stared down at the galantine. Apparently it was a big, stuffed fish smothered in aspic. Would there be no end to the evening's surprises?

Robbie gently removed the platter from my sagging arms. "It's right neighborly of you and Esau, Amos. Make yourself comfortable while I figure out how we can eat this."

Much later I wandered into my very own bedroom. I set down the candlestick atop the rosewood dresser and closed the door. A door to close. *Privacy*. Unbelievable. I began stripping off my clothes. I'd gotten past the shirt and boots and trousers and was fumbling with the tight cloth that bound my female attributes into acquiescence, as it were. As the final bonds were loosed, I sighed in relief.

*"Freedom,"* I whispered.

I raised my eyes. I saw what I'd missed before— a looking glass. Robbie had had a looking glass set over the little dresser. I hardly recognized either the face or figure revealed before me by the reflected light. An oval face surrounding big, green eyes. I fluttered my lashes. They were long and slightly curled. The nose wasn't bad, and the lips were full. My hair was thick and growing almost to the nape of my neck. I shook the short mane. Glints of mahogany red, with a touch of brassy gold, winked back at me. As for the rest of the body—I revolved experimentally before the mirror. . . . A woman. I was growing into a full-fledged woman. How was I to deal with this latest surprise?

I studied my image again. In fairness, it wasn't a true surprise. I was only now seeing what I'd begun feeling, but had been in no position to express—aside from that one long embrace in Robbie's arms the night he'd come into the tent so changed himself. Changed, yet still Robbie. Just as I was still Phoebe, underneath everything. Yet somehow *different*. I wrapped my arms about my body. He'd felt so good—

A soft tap sounded at the door. I dove for the discarded shirt to cover my discoveries with its ample linen.

"What is it?"

"It's just me, Feeb. I wanted to wish you good night."

I cracked the door open several inches. "Things are going to have to be just the same as before, Robbie. Maybe more so."

"I know, but—"

"But what, Robbie?"

"I just wanted you to know. . . ." He stopped and finally let out a tremendous sigh that seemed to travel all the way through his six-foot-plus frame. "It seemed like such a good idea. All this coming up in the world. All this space and all these fancy *things*. But I miss you already, Phoebe. I miss you lying in your bedroll so close. I miss reaching out and touching your hand."

"I understand, Robbie." What else could I say? I truly did understand that he was feeling these new emotions just as I was. Probably had been for some time, now that I considered the situation. But it was necessary to keep a cool head, to carry on with these new variations to our old masquerade.

Robbie was my partner. He was my best friend. He was also my protector. He'd always be my protector until I changed the rules. And growing or not, I knew it wasn't time to change them yet.

"Good night, Robbie." I closed the door and climbed into my fancy, cold bed.

# TEN

$\mathcal{S}$teamships from Panama filled with raucous gold seekers from the isthmus crossing had begun arriving in February. They were big steamships: the *California*, the *Oregon*, and the *Panama*. They kept arriving, each sighting setting off a round of celebratory cannon shots from the shore. Another thousand and more men swooped down on San Francisco. Even when the wet season ended and many took to the hills for the diggings, San Francisco continued to bustle and grow. There were ever more men arriving. Thirty houses a day were being raised in the hills and over the heights of the city. Business was never better.

On a warm day in May, Amos and I were sweating over our stoves. We weren't in a canvas tent anymore. Sam Brannan had footed the costs with us—forty-five–fifty-five—for the building of a genuine restaurant. It was two stories and took up about fifty feet of street frontage. We'd gone all out and built it across the way from the Parker House in the new Portsmouth Square. We were in good company. A U.S. Customs House had just risen down the street, and a post office, too. The Miner's Bank was already doing land-office business. I missed the breezes blowing through the gaps in the old canvas tent, though. I also missed serving regular customers three times the day. Our old sixty-dollars-the-week patrons had long since vamoosed for the hills. Our new ones were ever-changing, just like the city, and paid by the meal. The profits were no longer as extravagant, but they remained steady.

I straightened from the fancy sauce I'd been laboring over. Tastes were changing, too. The miners coming back from Sacramento and Coloma and Hangtown wanted luxuries—exotic tastes to match their newfound wealth. I longed for the simpler old days of pea soup, steaks, raw oysters, and eggs. The simpler days when I could joke with the customers, or make a showing of Papa's rifle—whichever was appropriate. Turning from the stove to reach for a big spoon sitting on the nearest counter, I tripped over Esau.

"Watch out, mutt!"

I hadn't said it that unkindly, but he acted hurt anyhow. I bent to scratch behind his ears. "Sorry, boy. I guess I'm a little short on patience these days."

Amos came bounding over to my stove to fuss. "You can't leave a sauce like this alone for a minute, Feeb. It'll just curdle and die on you!" He beat it rapidly, yelling over his shoulder, "Pixley! . . . Where is that sous-chef!"

"Here, sir!"

The latest addition to our kitchen came in a rush. He was a slim, sallow youth who'd lasted a month in the mining camps before giving up.

"Stir!" Amos commanded.

"Yes, sir, Mr. Amos!"

I watched Pixley stir, a harried combination of fearfulness and the desire to make good. It seemed as if everyone in San Francisco was like that these days. Trying so hard that it hurt. Scared silly they wouldn't move fast enough, accomplish enough, to keep up with the pretensions of the city. Afraid they were going to be left out of something.

Left out of what? I'd been working seven days a week for months, barely giving myself the time to notice all the new changes. Certainly not giving myself the opportunity to enjoy any of the money Robbie was busily investing or stashing away in the Miner's Bank for us. The money that still seemed too easy to be real. Nobody back home in Oregon would ever believe that Robbie and I had just been in the right place at the right time—willing to take the chance, willing to work.

I wiped my brow, then all of a sudden tore off my apron and reached for the frock coat hanging on a hook by the far wall. "Can you take over for a while, Amos? I need some air."

Amos was ladling one of his French sauces over a plate of veal cutlets, an attentive waiter standing to one side, ready to whisk the order into the dining room. "Out? You're going out in the midst of the dinner rush?"

My hand hovered over the coat, momentarily wavering. Then I steeled myself. If I could be decisive with my staff, I could learn to be decisive about my own needs, too. "Yes. I'm going *out*!"

"By all means. By all means! Esau and I will keep the fires burning."

"Thank you, Amos."

I stood blinking in the unaccustomed daylight of Portsmouth Square, staring across the dusty, open space at the veranda of the Parker House and the even newer hotels to either side. There was a long line of men snaking across the area between bustling carts and wagons, lining up for the post office. The monthly mail ship from the East must have arrived. Over to my left a California flag snapped in the wind high on its pole next to the customs house. Beyond, the bald hills around the city were still green—between their scattering of tents—after the spring rains.

Beneath me, my legs rocked slightly. It felt as if I'd just emerged from the hold of the brig *Oriental*. But that was years ago. *Lifetimes* ago. There was no way it could have been only seven months. I attempted to take a step, but only managed to sway. Against my will, dizziness began to overcome me, and my eyes began fluttering closed. A hand reached out to catch me as I fell.

"Repent, lad! Repent! Here's my hand to pull you from the flames of Hell!"

My eyes opened on a long-bearded man, dressed all in black. "What are you talking about?"

"About the dens of iniquity surrounding you! About the rum and whiskey mills you've obviously been frequenting! But the Lord has arrived in San Francisco at last, in the person of myself—the Reverend Ezekiel Wheeler. You're saved, lad!"

I shook my head and tried to struggle from his grasp. A temperance lecture in San Francisco? Now I knew for a certainty the entire world truly had arrived. "Thank you kindly, Reverend, but I've never touched the stuff—aside from testing one of my cook's Madeira sauces. I'm afraid I just felt poorly for a minute there."

He was loath to unhand me. "Delusion. This life is but a vale of tears and delusion, my son. Repent while the chance is yet yours!"

Politeness wasn't going to work. I broke loose to run across the square. Why hadn't Robbie warned me what all was transpiring outside?

I ended my flight down by the new wharves. A certain amount of commerce was occurring again, but it must have been hard going for the ships still sailing to maneuver between those abandoned hulls clogging the harbor. Most of them just stood off beyond and ferried goods and passengers by smaller boats. I lowered myself onto the raw boards of the pier so I could dangle my legs from the edge.

It was that crisp time of day between the morning fogs and the evening fogs, when a sharp wind seemed to sweep the clouds from sight for a few hours. Watching laborers unloading dories, listening to the shrieking calls of circling gulls, I began to breathe freely again. Why hadn't I escaped from the restaurant more often? Why hadn't I noticed that the gloss had long since worn off my little experiment? What was I trying to prove? And to whom?

A grunt from somewhere behind broke my thoughts and made the hairs at the nape of my neck tingle. It was a familiar grunt. Spare words followed.

"Feeb? Feeb. Come. Overbeam needs."

I spun around. "Olimpio?"

It was Olimpio—in his familiar buckskin trousers, and that elk-skin vest we'd made back in the cave. He was different, though. Thinner, his bronzed skin no longer gleaming with health. I jumped to my feet, wanting to hug him, but settling for a more brotherly slap on the back. He accepted the greeting with his usual stoicism.

"Where's Mr. Overbeam? What happened at El Dorado? Why are you in San Francisco? Why—"

He steered me from the wharf. "*Said* Overbeam bad cook. Poison himself. Almost me."

"Mr. Overbeam is sick? How did you find me? . . . Why . . . where . . . ?"

Olimpio refused to respond to any further conversational attempts. He was secure in his purpose and led me unfalteringly through the streets of the city to its poorest section, the hovels built of snippets of canvas and scrap where only those with the worst possible luck resided. Why on earth would Mr. Overbeam be living here? With that Mother Lode of his on Blackwater Creek, he should be able to afford the Parker House, at the least. Olimpio finally halted before a shanty and waved me inside. I went.

There was a filthy cot, a lantern, and a few

packs strewn about. Mr. Overbeam was lying on the cot, clutching his stomach. His top hat had fallen to the hard dirt floor, but his nightcap was yet intact. I knelt by his side and found myself praying for the first time in entirely too long. *Lord, this is one of the good people. One of your kind and gentle lambs. One of the innocents. Spare Mr. Overbeam, Lord.*

I touched his forehead. He was feverish. "Mr. Overbeam? Sir?"

He cranked open an eye. "Is that you, Feeb? Still in the Land of Dreams? Still treading the streets paved with gold? What happened to Oregon?"

"We never quite made it back, Robbie and I."

"I suspected as much. Sent Olimpio on a little tracking mission, just in case. He always was an exceptional tracker." He tried to move his head and the tassel of his nightcap jiggled feebly. "I've no other family, child."

"I know, Mr. Overbeam. Don't you fret. I'll get you up and running again."

His skinny hand flitted from his stomach to grasp mine. It was cold as death itself. "It may be too late."

His words wrenched at my own stomach, clear up to my heart. "It's never too late, Mr. Overbeam!

Have a little faith in yourself. And rest quiet now, because I'm going to take care of everything."

I stood up and turned to Olimpio. "Grab some of those men lounging around outside. Tell them there's a paying job. We've got to get him out of here!"

Four men carried Mr. Overbeam from that disastrous hovel. They carried him gently and well up the long hill to my home. Olimpio and I saw to that. They carried him across the veranda and into the hallway where Mrs. Meeks stood waiting in eternal vigilance over her twenty percent. Question marks rose all over her plump face. I didn't give her a chance to ask even one of those birthing thoughts.

"Send a bath to my rooms, with plenty of hot water. Send your boy out for a doctor. Send someone else to hunt for Robbie. Send word to Amos that I won't be back at the restaurant today, and he's in charge. . . . Don't just stand there clutching your lorgnette, Mrs. Meeks. I want it all done *now!*"

Up the two flights of stairs we climbed, directly to my bedroom. Mr. Overbeam was laid atop my four-poster bed. He opened his eyes for the first time during his journey. He managed one frail jerk of the tassel as he focused on the room.

"I see you've been diligent as always, young

Feeb. You've progressed in the world." He stopped. "But I can't be taking your fine bed—"

"Hush, Mr. Overbeam. Rest. I'll sleep on the couch."

I covered him with blankets and turned to Olimpio. "Make a fire for him, please. One in the sitting room, too. We've got to warm him up."

I paid the waiting men too much and sent them off. Then I walked to the windows of the sitting room to study the view over the bay that Robbie had bragged about on our own New Year's Eve. It was a fine view. A pity I'd been so busy I had to see it in daylight for the first time like this.

The doctor had come and gone. Mr. Overbeam's stomach had been purged. His body had been bathed. He lay now propped against my pillows, his person less substantial than ever without its layers, swallowed and lost within one of Robbie's nightshirts. Olimpio squatted on guard duty to one side of the bed. Robbie stood beside me at its foot, forgetting all pretense for the moment, clutching my hand.

"He looks a little better, Feeb."

"He does," I agreed. Then I began to worry again. "Do you think I was wrong, Robbie? Not allowing the doctor to dose him up with laudanum?

Or that calomel. I didn't like the looks of that blue stuff, either. Happy Hawkins back in Oregon always said herbs were best for anything that ails you. And she never lost a patient that I knew of."

My hand was squeezed again. "I'm sure Amos's herb poultice will help." Robbie smiled. "He near cleaned out the restaurant's spice shelf concocting it. Where I'm going to find all that thyme and rosemary and stuff for his sauces again, I just don't know."

I crept closer to the bed, pulling Robbie with me. Mr. Overbeam was beginning a gentle snore, like the purr of a cat. "Maybe he only needs to rest now."

"We do too, Feeb. It's been a long day."

I turned to the Indian. "You need more food, Olimpio? More blankets?"

He shook a no. "Olimpio fine. Watch Overbeam. Feeb and Robbie sleep."

We backed into the sitting room, softly closing the door. I moved past the fireplace to part the curtains of the windows overlooking the bay. San Francisco sprawled beneath us, lanterns twinkling here and there, columns of smoke rising slightly darker than the night sky.

"The wind is still for once," I whispered.

Robbie was at my side, and his hand slipped

around my waist. I leaned into him, needing his strength. "What are we doing here, Robbie? What are we accomplishing?"

"I always figured there was a reason for everything, Phoebe. Like the Bible says, 'To every thing there is a season, and a time to every purpose under heaven.' I figure I've already done the 'planting and plucking up' part. Even the 'time of war.' I'm waiting for the 'time to love.'"

His hand tightened around me, but I couldn't deal with that part now. "'A time to be born, and time to die, . . .'" I faltered to a stop. "It's not Mr. Overbeam's time yet, is it, Robbie?"

"I'm not sure, Phoebe. It's in the Lord's hands."

We stood like that well into the night.

"Who's absconded with my top hat? And my clothes! I'll have the rapscallion's liver for breakfast!"

Robbie and I dashed into the sickroom the next afternoon to find Mr. Overbeam wrestling with his covers. Olimpio towered over him, arms folded, a rare smile creasing his tight lips.

"Overbeam better."

Mr. Overbeam scowled from beneath the chaos he'd created. "Well? What have you scamps done with it all?"

I laughed. "Mrs. Meeks is having them laundered. You'll just have to be a good boy and rest until everything is clean again."

Overbeam growled. "Spoken like a true female, Feeb. You're going to have to face up to that little fact one of these days. Even Shakespeare let his women out of male disguise on occasion." He felt for his head. The familiar nightcap seemed to calm him. "But if you two want to keep playing your games, it's not my place to interfere. At least you didn't go and steal *this*," he muttered. Then his voice cranked up again. "And where's my breakfast? In an establishment of this opulence, a man should be served breakfast in bed."

"It's on its way, sir," Robbie answered. "From our restaurant. Amos is making you a special chicken broth."

"Broth!" Overbeam snarled. "Can't you see I need something more substantial than *broth*?"

Robbie and I exchanged glances and grins. It would seem the patient was going to live.

# ELEVEN

"*M*y faithful friend Olimpio and I survived the winter in fine fettle."

Mr. Overbeam was seated by the sitting room fire the next evening, once more safe within his layers of clothes. His feet were propped on one of those fancy stuffed footstools that'd come with the furniture. A very small glass of brandy for medicinal purposes was being warmed between his hands. Robbie and I lounged in chairs on either side of the fire, while Olimpio himself was sprawled on the upholstered settee, apparently taking great pleasure in its novelty.

"Alas, with the cessation of winter came the *forty-niners*. We forty-eighters were a different breed, my dear companions, a different breed. But a few brief months ago *honor* existed. *Respect* existed, and *dignity* and the ethical treatment of one's obvious territory—"

"What about Bog?" I asked pointedly. "You call his tactics ethical?"

Overbeam waved his glass. "A mere aberration. Never the norm. Bog and his cohorts were paragons of virtue compared to what invaded our hidden El Dorado a few short weeks ago."

Robbie stretched out his long legs. "What exactly happened, Mr. Overbeam?"

"What happened? What happened! Merely that Olimpio and I rose one morning to proceed to our diggings—only to find that we'd been invaded. Invaded by creatures talking *claims*! They must've been spying on us for days. There were dozens of them—pacing off sections of the Blackwater and marking them up with strings and little flags. '*Claims?*' said I. 'How can you talk claims? This whole valley is mine!'"

"What happened next, Mr. Overbeam?"

"Olimpio fetched his bow and arrows, Feeb. But there were too many. And they had guns." He downed the last of his brandy. "Too many."

We stared at the empty glass in his hands for a long time. It was Robbie who broke the silence.

"We can get you and Olimpio back on your feet, Mr. Overbeam. Feeb and I, we've got a good, profitable restaurant, and this lodging house, and a few other little investments. You're welcome to shares, both of you. Just like you offered us quarters of your gold vein."

"Robbie's right," I agreed. "Without our piece of Bog's money to get to San Francisco, we couldn't have organized all this."

"Bless you, children. I knew you could be relied upon. However—" Mr. Overbeam began to giggle. Behind him Olimpio snickered.

"I don't see what's so funny about offering you a piece of our hard-earned profits, Mr. Overbeam. Robbie and I sweated mightily for it all."

Mr. Overbeam rubbed at his nose, then roared outright. Robbie and I waited uncomfortably for him to settle down. When he finally finished wiping tears from his eyes with his nightcap tassel, he was capable of speech once more.

"I'm not insulting you, my dear Feeb, my dear giant. Never. But kindly allow me to proceed. Olimpio"—he glanced back at his partner—"being an Indian of some guile and infinite intelligence, noted the claim proceedings—and claimed for us what was left, what was unwanted."

"What might that have been, Mr. Overbeam?" Robbie was sitting up straight now. "If those scoundrels got the creek and the cliffs beyond with your vein—"

"Why, the cabin and the garbage pit, of course." Mr. Overbeam was chuckling again. "Even the greatest bounder would concede the cabin as mine.

And who'd want a garbage pit?"

To the rear, Olimpio actually guffawed.

I was beginning to lose patience. "Enough games, Mr. Overbeam. What was in the garbage pit?"

"Nothing but all those rusting tins—and the entire contents of our Mother Lode, my dear Feeb. Carefully secreted from the eyes of all. Nothing but that."

"The vein ran dry?"

"Alack, but a few days previous. We'd managed to work it for a good month before the interlopers arrived. Loath as I was to give up my lovely valley, Olimpio and I had been hard-pressed to devise a means of transporting the gold back to civilization—such as it is—before the claim seekers arrived with their wagons and burros and horses."

"And?" My impatience was mounting, making me testy. Had he got the gold out? What had he done with it? Why had I discovered him in such abject poverty?

"The obvious occurred, my dear Feeb. I traded the cabin for a thousand dollars' worth of dust, a wagon, and a string of animals, led by our staunch Romeo and Juliet, and their youngster, Tybalt."

"Tybalt?" I interrupted. "Juliet had a baby?"

"An infant of some charm," Mr. Overbeam veri-fied. "But to proceed. We managed to lodge all the samples in the Miner's Bank before some spring mushrooms I injudiciously harvested en route brought me to the depths of misery in which you found me."

I tugged at my hair in frustration. "But why didn't you spend some of it for a decent hotel room, Mr. Overbeam? And a doctor?"

"Spend my hard-earned gains on fripperies, Feeb? Spend your share? And Robbie's? Spend that which could be used to purchase my dearest dream, the original works of Shakespeare himself?"

Robbie and I groaned in unison.

"You wouldn't have needed Shakespeare's folio in heaven, Mr. Overbeam," I finally managed to choke out. "You could have chewed the ear off the man himself!"

"That is a thought." He pulled at his tassel. "Never even crossed my mind." He smiled. "It'll give me something to look forward to, won't it? In my declining years."

His answer did not appease me. "What about in the meantime, Mr. Overbeam. What do you intend to do *now*?"

"Why, inspect your San Francisco, of course. Perhaps purchase some new attire—from the skin out. And then I believe I'll take you up on Oregon City. Your various descriptions have made it sound more congenial to me as a permanent abode than this tempestuous town."

Olimpio grunted. "Oregon have mountains? Trees? Game?"

"Lots of all of them, Olimpio," I answered. "More than in California."

"Olimpio go, too."

I considered. And why not? Olimpio had enough dignity and intelligence to defend himself from any leftover Indian-haters in the Territory. Besides, he could keep an eye on Mr. Overbeam.

"You'll need contacts. Both of you. I'll write up some letters of introduction. To my parents, of course. And my sister's husband, Wade Jennings— he's the editor of *The Oregon Intelligencer* and would certainly be interested in your experiences for publication purposes. And Miss Simpson, who runs the Young Ladies' Seminary . . ." I faltered, suddenly missing Oregon for the first time in months.

"Don't forget Dr. McLoughlin," Robbie contributed. Then he added in explanation, "Before he retired, McLoughlin was Chief Factor at Fort Vancouver, sort of the unofficial governor of the entire Territory. The Great White Eagle and Mr.

Overbeam might enjoy each other."

And so we planned for Mr. Overbeam and Olimpio's future. Curious, but even yet it didn't occur to me to travel home with them. I may have been weary of Mother Phoebe's, but I wasn't sure where home was anymore.

Robbie and I saw Mr. Overbeam and Olimpio off on a bright June day. The Oregon schooner had unloaded her cargo quickly, anxious to be off to sea again before her sailors got gold dust in their eyes. The ship took our friends, but left something, as well. It was a letter for me from home. My first connection to everything I'd escaped from last autumn. I clutched the missive in one hand as I waved good-bye to our companions with the other. The ship's boat wound its way between rotting vessels in the bay until our friends were out of sight. I collapsed onto the wharf.

"What is it, Feeb? What does it say?" Robbie lowered himself beside me.

"Give me half a chance, Robbie." I tore at the envelope and slipped out the sheaf of papers. The letter was in Mama's hand. Just seeing that made me want to jump up and cry out for Overbeam's dory to return for me. Instead, I reached for the vast masculine handkerchief in my pocket and blew my nose noisily. My eyes finally cleared enough for me to take in the words.

"Everybody's fine. . . . Papa's taken on a hired hand. . . . Amelia's pregnant. . . ." I stopped. "Amelia's going to have a baby! My big sister!"

"When?" Robbie asked reasonably.

"Hush . . ." My eyes skimmed over the writing. "In September. And she's already starting to show." I shuffled back to the first page. "Mama wrote this the end of April. Amelia must be big by now. . . . And Miss Prendergast—Mrs. Judd—is expecting again. And—I don't believe it!"

"What, Feeb?" Robbie was eating up my news as if it were *his* friends and family it was all about.

"Margaret O'Malley's been seen walking with a young man after church of a Sunday." I pulled my head up from the page to explain. "Margaret was my best friend from the Trail, Robbie. And her big sister, Lizzie—she's Amelia's friend—Lizzie's had a baby boy. With red hair and freckles! . . . And the Kennan twins, Hannah and Sarah—they're these gorgeous blondes that kept falling in love with Indians from every tribe we bumped into along two thousand miles? Well, they haven't married yet at all!"

"Where's the news in that, Feeb?"

I gave Robbie the eye. "If you'd ever seen the Kennan twins, you'd understand, Robbie."

"But I haven't, and I don't."

"Never mind." I finished running through the letter. "And Mama says Papa is still angry with me for taking off like I did, but appreciates the money I sent with the last letter and has already forwarded it by ship back East to order that reaper machine I suggested. He hopes to have it delivered within the next two years. And . . ." My voice choked off and I started dabbing at my eyes again.

"What else does it say, Feeb?"

I took a deep breath, trying to control my feelings. "Mama says she's still praying for me every single hour of every day. And she's glad I'm doing so well, but"—I stopped to have another go at my nose—"she hopes I'll come home again in her lifetime."

"Your mama's not that old, Feeb!"

"I know, Robbie!" I gave up right then and there for a truly good bawl.

Robbie sat next to me, wanting to comfort me, but not being able to on account of it was such a public place. I noticed that, too, between onslaughts of tears. Unnatural is what this whole situation was turning into. . . . When a young man couldn't comfort a young lady in her time of need, because the young lady was disguised by trousers. . . . I bawled harder.

# TWELVE

*M*r. Overbeam's coming and going caused changes. Perhaps it had something to do with my quarter share from his Mother Lode sitting in the Miner's Bank—at least the piece of it I hadn't sent home with him for my parents. Then again, maybe the changes were just sitting there waiting to happen. In any event, I began to run Mother Phoebe's a little differently.

I got me some fancy embroidered waistcoats like Robbie's and turned the kitchen over to Amos and his growing staff of apprentice cooks. I'd never be able to devise a champagne sauce or roast a truffled turkey or make jug hare, English style, the way Amos could. It was time to stop fooling myself. The days of flapjacks and pea soup were over for good in San Francisco.

What San Francisco wanted now was elegance and style. Accordingly, I gave up on serving breakfasts along with running the rear of the restaurant. I took over the front. In between graciously greeting customers in my new finery, I devised highfalutin

menus that Robbie had printed up. I got rid of
the long tables and replaced them with intimate
ones, suitable for businessmen desiring to discuss
their latest deals in some privacy. I reorganized the
upstairs into cozy rooms swathed in velvet so the
women beginning to arrive by ship could dine out
with their husbands. I took long breaks for fresh
air and began to accompany Robbie on some of his
rounds.

No wonder Robbie had been having such a
good time all these months. He was the one who'd
got to hobnob with the business leaders of San
Francisco. He was the one who'd been able to greet
the latest ships from Mexico, or the islands, or even
China—and to cozen them out of their luxuries—
for a price. Mother Phoebe's had real china plates
now, and settings of silver. I had to keep an eagle
eye on that cutlery, though. There were still some
not beneath pocketing a few pieces to trade for play
in the monte parlors.

I was crouched over a corner table one day in
early July struggling over a new menu—the prices
changed so quickly these days—trying to figure out
Frenchified names for things.

"Hey, Amos!" I yelled at the curtains screening
the kitchen from the dining room. It was between
meals and only a few patrons lingered, so I could

act like we were still in the old tent.

His head popped out. "Yes, Feeb?"

"What'd you say the French was for *chicken*?"

"Poolay. *P-o-o*—"

I started scratching down *p-o-o*.

"Pardon for the intrusion, but—"

I glanced from my labors to the male form now hovering expectantly over me. Mid thirties he was, with a certain gauntness of cheek and a hairline beginning to recede. Distinguished, yet frayed at the edges. I kind of took to the way he'd said that first word . . . *par-dawn*.

"You discuss *la cuisine française*, monsieur?" he continued. "Perhaps I might be of assistance."

I smiled. "It's all the rage now. Any well-sauced dish has to have a French name. And they're all well sauced these days—wine sauce, cream sauce, cheese sauce. Trouble is, I can't spell them!"

"*Poulet. P-o-u-l-e-t*. Zis is your chicken."

"Have a seat, mister." I pushed out a chair with my foot. Never was one to turn down opportunity knocking. "Amos? Fetch some coffee for us, please? Now, then, just how would you attack the Rochambeau part of this poulet's sauce?"

That's how Jean-Luc came to be part of our little restaurant family. He was a musician by trade and had discovered that mining was not conducive to playing the violin. All that cold river water froze up his tendons, or something. Shortly thereafter, we had regular concerts of music at dinner and supper both. We also had properly spelled menus.

Not that there wasn't entertainment to be had at other establishments. These were, as Mr. Overbeam might have put it, of a more tempestuous nature, however. A good many men would go out of their way for questionable displays by scantily clad "ladies." Our clientele grew and prospered on class. Word got around to other hungry musicians, too, and soon Robbie had to find a piano.

Robbie and I sat listening to a concert one evening toward the end of August. Around us diners discreetly relished their meals. No more feeding at the trough at Mother Phoebe's. My partner sighed.

"What is it, Robbie?"

"Ain't this all just so *elegant*, Feeb?"

His fingers toyed unconsciously with the fob dangling over his extravagant waistcoat. That fob had done the final trick with his knuckle cracking, right enough. Just as I'd secretly suspicioned when I gave it to him.

"I can hardly believe it's ours. That *we* did it."

"Well, we did do it, Robbie. You and I together."

"You're right. Yet . . . there's one thing Mother Phoebe's still needs."

My eyes shot around the room. Bright linen tablecloths reached almost to the floor, and they were *not* done-over sheets. The floor itself was polished and clean. Fluted glasses sparkled with champagne. A few paintings of big European mountains decorated the wallpaper. Robbie had taken a fancy to them and bought them from a sea captain. Light shone from crystal wall sconces that only I and the dishwashers knew were so desperately hard to keep clean. Jean-Luc and Bill, the piano player, and some new addition with his legs wrapped around an overgrown fiddle he called a violoncello were playing their hearts out. They genteelly produced something that sounded like heaven, but Jean-Luc assured me was written by a long-dead gentleman named Mozart. I took in my world and saw that it was good.

"What could Mother Phoebe's possibly need, Robbie? It's practically perfect right now."

Robbie's hand edged toward mine, before remembering to behave itself. "Practically perfect isn't the same as perfect. It needs a *woman*. It needs *Phoebe*."

"Are you out of your mind?"

His fingers slipped up to his forehead, as if checking.

"Don't think so."

He smiled, and that smile made him look so handsome, I found myself sucking in my breath. Where had that farm boy from a long-ago Fourth of July celebration gone? And the skeletal soldier coming home from the Cayuse Wars? Or the young man who'd been stripped and scourged for me? They were still all there, of course, but they'd filled out and transformed themselves remarkably.

"There are women in San Francisco now, Phoebe. Legitimate women. Why, even Jessie Frémont was through last month chasing after her hero husband. It was in the papers."

"She dined here, Robbie. Sat right over there." I pointed. "A pretty little thing, younger than I expected. And dressed so fine—"

"Exactly, Phoebe. Wouldn't you like to do that, too? Don't you think it's past time? Long past time?"

Robbie had caught me for certain. All those mixed feelings that had been going through me these past few months—especially after Mr. Overbeam's unexpected little lecture—came to the fore. To be truly myself again. Wouldn't that be something?

"There'll be a price to pay, Robbie."

"What kind of a price?"

"What happens when Sam Brannan finds out? I signed our contract as a male."

"California's got new laws, Feeb. I've been following them. Women have property rights here now, not like in Oregon." He stopped. "Besides, he wouldn't have the nerve to cause a fuss. Not after what you've gone and done. The only thing Brannan is truly interested in is the profit. And you've given him a profit no sane man could complain about."

"You may have a point about Brannan, Robbie. Still . . ." There was something else. It was difficult, but I finally got it out. "How about us? What'll it do to us? People are going to talk. There'll be gossip—"

Robbie shrugged his shoulders. "Us is between us. Until you give the word it will be the same. Just like it always has been. The rest of the town I don't care about. San Francisco isn't Oregon City, Feeb. It's got a different set of values. People can be whoever they want to be here. They can even be themselves."

The piece Jean-Luc had been leading stopped. A sudden silence overtook the room, to be replaced by polite applause and the low buzz of conversation. I pulled at my waistcoat and rearranged the ruffles of my shirt. "Give me a little time to think about it, Robbie. I need to think."

I chose my sixteenth birthday for my San Francisco debut. It seemed appropriate. Hadn't another kind of rebirth happened upon the same occasion three long years ago in the Blue Mountains? My image shimmering in the looking glass over my bedroom dresser shivered in remembrance. A mortally wounded mama grizzly had toppled over me, smothering me close to death in her final embrace. Since I had done the mortal wounding, her revenge seemed appropriate, if somewhat unacceptable to myself. Still, I had survived the grizzly. Surely I could survive San Francisco society.

*Ugh.* I tugged at the new kind of restraints imposed upon me. It had been necessary to let some female in on my game so as not to shock the good cloth merchants and tailors of the town. Mrs. Meeks being the only female of my acquaintance, she'd received the dubious honor of my confessions.

"La!" the woman had exclaimed. "All is now explained. The flowers at table, the china, even the music. Only the tender sensibilities of the fairer sex could devise such prettiments."

"That's as it may be, Mrs. Meeks, but what do I do next?"

"Next?" She raised her lorgnette to her eyes and peered at me for a long time, as if working out the new differences. "Next, my dear, we shall measure you for appropriate unmentionables."

Now I studied the unmentionable currently imprisoning me. Almost as bad as my chest binding it was—only it worked to the opposite purpose. Goodness, how it worked. It was a genuine Paris woven corset, with front-fastening stays. It was also strapless, stiff with whalebone, and shaped to the breasts. Then there were the drawers, and the camisole, and the crinoline petticoats. So many things to deal with before covering them all with the main event—the dress.

My year in disguise as a male was beginning to feel desirable again. Such simple, workable clothes men wore. Maybe I didn't have to do this. Maybe things could just go on indefinitely as they'd been. . . .

Robbie knocked at my bedroom door. "How's it going in there? It's almost time for the supper sitting at the restaurant."

"Have a little patience, Robbie! It takes a while for a butterfly to break free of its cocoon."

"I can hardly manage it"—his voice was a low

purr through the barrier that separated us—"but I'll wait, Phoebe. Indeed, I will!"

I glanced another time into the looking glass. I suppose I could blame this all on Robbie. His patience with our charade did seem to be wearing thin at last. No. I ought to be more honest than that. My patience was wearing thin, too. The trouble was, I wanted things both ways—the ease of being a male along with the honor of being a woman. It was just so much more *trouble* being a woman.

I gritted my teeth, made a first attempt at bending within the whalebones, and ultimately managed to get myself into the dress. Afraid to look at the final transformation, I strode into the sitting room, almost tripping on the skirts before remembering I could no longer *stride*, but must develop a sort of mincing step. That annoyed me, too, along with another impossibility of high-toned female attire—buttons. Those last few buttons down my back that I would never be able to reach and as a result were still undone. What could possibly make up for all this inconvenience? Growling beneath my breath, I made a halfhearted pirouette before the fireplace and my partner.

"You'll have to deal with these rear neck buttons, Robbie. I can see right now a woman needs a maid if she's to go out in public."

Robbie stood away from the fire to stare. For a long time. His eyes registered pleasure and wonder. "I don't believe in maids, Phoebe. Wouldn't a husband do?"

A *husband*? My foul humor evaporated as my body settled itself within its new finery. My arms felt suddenly light as a butterfly's wings. The chest which had been so ignominiously hidden for months swelled. So did my sudden smile. Maybe there was something to be said for liberating the female form. I do believe Robbie was proposing! "He would if there were proper husband material around," I teased. "And if I were a little older."

Robbie pulled something from his waistcoat pocket. "My ma married at sixteen, Phoebe."

Somehow that wasn't what I'd expected next. What had I expected? For Robbie to get down on his knees before me? He wasn't that kind of a person. He'd proven himself in other ways. But even if he had gone and turned all soppy on me, my answer would have been the same. "I'm not your ma, Robbie."

"Don't I know that! I knew your answer, too, or this would've been a ring." In his hand was a gleaming golden necklace—a chain with a jewel dangling from it.

I floated closer to the glitter, inexplicably attracted. "What is it, Robbie?"

"It's a birthday present. I had the chain done up from part of Mr. Overbeam's Mother Lode, as a kind of remembrance. And the bauble part, why, that's an emerald, to match your eyes, and the green of your dress."

He closed the distance still between us, slipped the necklace over my head, then bent to fasten the final pearl buttons down my back. I wasn't sure how he managed it, his fingers were so thick, and the pearls so tiny.

"Happy birthday, Phoebe." Lips brushed the nape of my neck, sending my entire spine into tingles. "I'm very happy you did this thing."

His kindness was becoming overpowering. His presence was, too. Why hadn't our year together prepared me for this? Why hadn't I sensed what would be waiting for me outside of my cocoon? I shook the necklace until it settled on my chest, gleaming.

"Thank you, Robbie. It *is* lovely." I was afraid to turn back toward him, afraid one look into his eyes would transform me again, to stone—or something else equally un-Phoebe-like.

"Let's get this over with." Head high, skirts raised, I marched out the door as if going to my execution.

# THIRTEEN

*A* daguerreotype parlor had invaded San Francisco. It was the latest rage. Everyone who was anyone—and all the rest of us, too—made appointments to have our images done up for posterity. In my case, it was more for Mama and Papa, to prove to them that I was truly alive and well. Of course, Robbie came along for the experience.

On the appointed day we presented ourselves in suitable costume. Robbie had gotten the idea into his head that he wanted a portrait of us together—both before and after my most recent transformation. That meant I had to get back into my old clothes of disguise. It wasn't that much of a hardship. Since my debut I'd come to the unalterable opinion that the only place whalebone belonged was on a whale. Still, I stuck to my new role. It did seem to tickle people so.

Pulling on the fawn trousers in the daguerreotypist's changing room, my mind went back to that first night at Mother Phoebe's. My birthday night. I certainly had caused an uproar. You'd think it was the second coming of the gold rush the way folks acted.

First off was Esau. He started in racing toward me when he heard my voice from his usual spot under a stove in the kitchen. Well into the dining room, two feet before he hit my skirts, he skidded to a stop in mid gallop. He landed plop on his rear quarters in confusion. Next he lifted his hairy little head, cocked both ears, and barked.

"What's the matter, mutt? Don't you know who I am?"

He yelped again, before embarking on a full circuit of my skirts, sniffing each inch of the hem. At last deciding that I was Feeb after all, he made a flying leap for my arms and went straight for the emerald.

"Sorry, *not* that." Esau met the floor again and whined his bewilderment.

"What's going on out there?" Amos stuck his curly gray head through the curtains. "Bless me. What brought this on, Feeb? Surely you've been under a strain lately, but—"

Our diners were taking in the tableau with unadulterated interest. Robbie—standing by with a sappy grin on his face—finally came to my rescue.

"Gentlemen, it is my distinct pleasure to

introduce to you the one and only, the genuine,
Mother Phoebe. At last!"

From his little dais, Jean-Luc made a flourish
with his violin. "*Mais, c'est parfait!* My congratu-
lations, Mademoiselle Phoebe. A thousand felicita-
tions! All is now as it should be."

The audience—that is, our patrons, though it
certainly felt as if I were on a stage—burst into
rousing applause, and a few catcalls. I blushed clear
down my neckline. And it continued like that all
evening.

The remembrance turned me to blushing again
as I settled back into my old ruffled shirt and
waistcoat and trousers. It stayed with me as I was
seated in the daguerreotypist's studio chair. A
brace clamped my neck firmly in place, but it did
nothing to quell all the second and third thoughts
about my transformation spinning wildly through
my head. Robbie stood stolidly behind me, one
hand resting comradelike on my shoulder. The
master of this modern form of torture hovered
behind his camera.

"You must remain *absolutely* still for a full minute. Try not to even close your eyes. . . . Not yet!
Breathe freely for a moment. Grasp air within your
lungs . . ." His head disappeared behind his appa-
ratus, and finally a muffled voice was heard. "Now!"

Robbie and I froze for an eternity. All the days of my life within this costume, this character, flashed before me. The good days in San Francisco, the bad days in Papa's trousers in El Dorado and in the cave . . . which hadn't really been so bad . . . the long walk of escape from the homestead to Astoria before smuggling ourselves aboard the brigantine *Oriental* . . .

"You may breathe! It is accomplished!"

I breathed.

"Time to change, Phoebe."

"What?" I blinked distractedly.

"For the next picture."

I sat again in a dress with Robbie. Then I sat in the dress by myself. This would be the picture for Mama and Papa. More thoughts flew through my head as the sixty seconds turned into another lifetime. My days as a member of the Petticoat Party on the Oregon Trail flashed by. Days learning to do a man's job while still dressed in calico skirts. Then there were the days on Papa's homestead, fussing and fuming with Papa and the oxen both, in that same calico while I searched hopelessly for freedom. Other days in skirts, days that were better, flashed back to me. Like that Fourth of July dance where I'd met Robbie. We'd danced, sure enough, but we'd also got in a little target practice as well.

I'd really done a remarkable amount of things as a girl before my days of even greater freedom as a young man in the gold rush. So why was it so hard on me being a girl again? No, not a *girl* anymore. A *woman*. Maybe it all came down to that—

"Breathe again, please!"

I sighed. The portraits were completed. The entire ritual. And I remained in total confusion.

Robbie and I left the studio. He was assured, jaunty, comfortable with himself and what had transpired. I was feeling as wrecked as those abandoned ships beginning to rot and sink in the bay.

"We'll have to do that once a year, Phoebe. At the least. A wonderful thing is modern science."

"Why in the world, Robbie? It was torture, pure and simple. And we paid for it!"

He broke off the whistle he'd begun and halted in the middle of the street we'd been crossing. I stopped with him, and two wagons had to detour around us, curses on the lips of their drivers.

"You've been acting mighty strange lately, Phoebe."

"Me? Strange! Since when?"

"Since, since . . ."

He considered carefully, ignoring several horses and a string of mules completely. Robbie had always had that ability to focus in absolutely straight lines. Straight to the finish. Me looking like a girl again signified the obvious to him—marriage. He'd never be able to conceive that to *me* becoming suddenly attractive, suddenly feminine, was more on the order of throwing a pebble into a pond and watching the circles keep spreading, infinitely. . . . Well, if he wanted to debate all this in the middle of a muddy San Francisco street, that was all right with me. I dropped the skirts I'd been hoisting over the sludge. I'd never been a stranger to dirt, either. Let Mrs. Meeks and her laundresses figure how to get it all out.

"How long have I been acting strange? Say it, Robbie!"

"Well, since you went back to being a girl."

"That was partly your idea, Robbie. Admit it!"

"True enough, but I never expected it to turn you all ornery and difficult and—"

Fussing over my new clothes, suddenly expecting men not to expectorate in the environs of my skirts or blow cigar smoke in my face was being ornery and difficult? Then again, maybe he was referring to these little differences of opinion we'd begun having lately. I stared up, way up into his eyes. "Ornery and difficult and *what*, Robbie?"

"Irresistible and *female*, blast it!"

My mind sailed right past that irresistible part.

"And what exactly did you anticipate, Robbie Robson? You can't have it both ways. Unless you expect me to act *neuter* for the rest of my life!"

He rubbed a splattering of muck—a gift of passing wagon wheels—from his cheek. "Tarnation. That's not what I meant at all, atall—"

"Out of the way, you idiots!"

"Coming through!"

I grabbed Robbie's arm and hauled him to the far side of the street at last. We stood on the board walk glaring and trying to rub mud from our clothing. We only ground it in worse. I finally spoke.

"You can tell Amos I'll be late to work. I've got to go home to change my dress."

"What about our portraits?"

"You can pick them up whenever they're ready. And then I don't care what you do with them, Robbie."

But I did care. Late the next night I stood staring at the brass-framed images Robbie had carefully positioned upon the mantelpiece over the fire before stalking off to his room. We hadn't really spoken to each other for going on two days now. Only necessary things within the restaurant. Things like "We need another hundred pounds of Brannan's veal" (me), or "Can't you ask Jean-Luc to play something with a *tune* in it sometimes?" (Robbie).

The pictures stared back at me from beneath their protective glass, changing from negative to positive depending on how you looked at them in the flickering light. Negative and positive, the two different sides of our natures, the two different sides of our friendship. Perhaps the wonders of modern science could show us something new. Something more than the obvious.

At least our eyes were open. That was a wonder. Some results of sittings I'd seen had closed eyes—as if the portraits were of sleepers, or the dead. But there we were, right enough, almost alive in miniature. Robbie big and solid and impossibly solemn. Me looking a little scared. I studied them closer. I looked more scared in the dress than in the pants. I truly did.

I glanced down at my nightgown, then quickly stepped back to keep its cloth from the fire's sparks. I felt better now, neither in trousers nor in whalebone and crinolines. I'd probably feel best in *nothing,* the way I was acting these days. But San Francisco didn't have the climate for that. I hugged my arms to my body.

Who was I these days? Feeb or Phoebe Brown? And what did either of these persons have to do with San Francisco, and Robbie? What did they have to do with the Oregon Territory?

Oregon was hard to even remember anymore. All that struggle to get from the East on the Oregon Trail with the Petticoat Party. All that struggle merely to remain alive. Was being in San Francisco and having more money than I knew what to do with the answer to anything? Surely there was more to life. . . . Like learning how to properly become a woman, now that I'd taken on the trappings of one. In all my sixteen years, there'd never really been time for learning that. For getting used to the idea of my inherent femininity. And connected to that was learning what to do about my chaotic feelings over Robbie—feelings that changed from day to night and back again as fast as these daguerreotype portraits went from positive to negative.

I needed some advice badly. Female advice. Not just from Mrs. Meeks, either. Advice from females I truly knew and trusted. Women who'd maybe already gone through what I was suddenly going through. And the only women who really fit that description were Mama and my big sister, Amelia.

"Feeb. Phoebe."

Robbie had crept up on me, unannounced.

"I'm sorry for today, Phoebe. And yesterday,

too. It's only that sometimes—" His waistcoat was off, and his collar open at the neck. He pulled at it. "Sometimes I have a little trouble understanding you, Phoebe."

"Sometimes I have a little trouble myself, Robbie."

"Forgive me?"

"That's easy enough to do, Robbie. It's forgiving myself that's harder."

He reached out a hand to my arm. "Let me help you. I'll do anything. . . ."

I touched his lingering hand with my own. "I know, Robbie. But I've got to do it for myself. Got to figure things out for myself." I gently brushed off his warm fingers.

"What's that supposed to mean?"

Of a sudden, I knew. It became so obvious. "I think I have to go back to Oregon, Robbie. I *know* I have to. To deliver this picture to Mama and Papa personally. To talk to my sister, Amelia, see her new baby—"

"I'll go with you, Phoebe."

"No. It's something I need to do on my own."

"By yourself? But we've done everything together, Phoebe. Shared everything!"

"So we have." I smiled at him. "But this part,

well . . . I believe I have to finish growing up on my own, Robbie."

His hand moved to my cheek. "So your mind is set. And when your mind is set, there's nothing that'll change it. I've learned that much about you, at the least." He tried to return my smile, but it wasn't convincing. "I'll wait any amount of time for the growing, Phoebe. Any amount. But I would like to be there while it's happening."

I reached for his own cheek, rough to my smooth. "I know you would, Robbie. Give me credit for understanding that. But there's the business here for you to look after."

Now he broke away from my touch, as if it hurt. He leaned next to the fireplace for support, mussed his thick crop of hair. "I figured it might come to this."

I watched the light glance off the yellow of his head. "I'll miss you, Robbie. I truly will."

# FOURTEEN

*M*aybe it was fate. The brigantine *Oriental* was the next Oregon-bound ship in harbor. Captain Fallows himself was still in command. He didn't recognize me as I shipped on.

"Miss Brown, a distinct honor to have ye aboard my humble vessel!"

His squat figure bent over my gloved hand and he actually kissed it! I suppressed a giggle. "About accommodations, Captain?"

"Yes, yes. I have a fine cabin fitted. And ye shall dine at my own table. The seas are calm for late October. I expect to give ye a comfortable voyage."

"Thank you, Captain." Money certainly could make a difference. Apparently at least that part of my reputation had preceded me. "As for these—" My arm gracefully swooped to take in the vast pile of presents and luggage I'd acquired for my journey.

"My sailors shall see to everything, Miss Brown. Your possessions shall be treated with all respect due."

"Again, thank you." I swept to the rails. "Shall we depart soon?"

"Within minutes. The tides are with us. The winds are good."

"You may leave me, Captain."

The old villain scuttled off and I leaned into the rails, breathing in the last of the San Francisco smells. Memorizing the clutter of masts and the city beyond as if it were my last sighting. Within me, my heart beat so hard I could hardly keep up my latest masquerade. I was truly leaving San Francisco. Truly leaving Robbie.

Earlier on the wharf Robbie had actually wept. He hadn't cared two pennies for the crowd of sailors and laborers surrounding us. Just fished out his huge handkerchief—from the set with his initials embroidered in the corner that I'd given him as a present—and mopped at his eyes.

"It ain't going to be the same at all, Phoebe. Not at all."

He wasn't about to let me depart scot-free. I didn't even want him to. It would make what we'd gone through together trivial. And it hadn't been. None of it. "I know it won't be the same. That's part of the reason I'm leaving, Robbie. So things will have a chance to become different."

"So you say." He finally stuffed the damp handkerchief back in a pocket. "As long as they don't become completely different. Promise me you'll come back, Phoebe."

"I'm not making any promises whatsoever, Robbie. I wish I could, but I can't. I only know that I'll think of you every day . . . every hour."

The sailors holding the dory for me began to fidget uncomfortably.

"I've got to go now, Robbie. The tide waits for no man." I smiled. "Or woman."

Robbie grabbed me for a parting kiss. He aimed for my cheek, but missed when I turned my head slightly. I'd like to believe that it wasn't on purpose that I turned my head that way. I was trying to prove my independence, after all. But the fact remains that I did consciously move toward him.

His lips landed on mine. An entire year that had taken. Sweet and good is how they felt lingering over the opportunity. I began to wonder what I'd been fighting so long as I leaned into his embrace. The moment just naturally extended itself and thoughts came back to me from long before. Birthing thoughts on first seeing the great Columbia River three years back—about what might happen if I ever met a young man as deep and strong and masculine as that river.

"Time, ma'am," one of the sailors finally broke in.

*Time?* Already? When I'd only now discovered the depths being offered to me? I extricated myself from my partner's arms. With difficulty.

"Be good, Robbie."

I wanted to say a world of other things. I wanted to stay. But I was already being handed into the boat.

Here I stand at the last, alone. Staring back in the direction of that wharf. In the direction of Robbie. Wondering again. Above me the sails are filling with wind. The ship is plowing off into it, as into a race, bound for Oregon.

*The*
# PETTICOAT PARTY
*Series:*

Read the first three books in the
# PETTICOAT PARTY
series:

## Petticoat Party Book 1:
## Go West, Young Women!

Sleeping under a wagon, eating moldy beans, and driving oxen through a dusty desert—nobody ever said the Oregon Trail was going to be like this! But just when twelve-year-old Phoebe Brown is sure she can't stand another day of her father and the other bossy men in the wagon train, a stampede of buffalo puts the women and girls in charge. The Oregon Trail will never be the same!

## Petticoat Party Book 2:
## **Phoebe's Folly**

Just beginning the final leg of their trek to Oregon City, the intrepid Petticoat Party is now properly armed with rifles—and the know-how to use them. But a rash remark from Phoebe about the women's prowess with firearms gets the party in trouble— and before they know it, they've been challenged to a shooting contest by a band of Snake Indians. Single-handedly, Phoebe manages to change the Wild West, not to mention the course of American history!

Petticoat Party Book 3:
## Oregon, Sweet Oregon

After weeks of hair-raising adventures on the Oregon Trail, Phoebe Brown and the intrepid Petticoat Party wagon train have finally arrived in Oregon City, the so-called Promised Land. After just a few days of plowing sod and chopping down trees, though, Phoebe finds Oregon less than promising—in fact, it's downright boring! Phoebe misses those exciting days of stampeding buffalo, lovesick Indians, and near starvation. And something terrible has happened to the rest of the Petticoat Party—they're all marrying and settling down to a life of farming. Have all Phoebe's adventures come to an end? Isn't there anyone else in Oregon who wants some excitement?